Disney

CHARMING
TALES

This Edition Exclusive to:

INNOVAGE

(949) 587-9207

Produced and published by

INNOVAGE, Inc.

19511 Pauling
Foothill Ranch, California,
92610
Tel: (949) 587-9207
Fax: (949) 587-9024

Printed in CHINA

CONTENTS

Walt Disney's

Snow White
and the Seven Dwarfs

Once upon a time there lived a lovely little princess named Snow White who lived with her stepmother, a beautiful but vain queen.

The Queen didn't want anyone to be more beautiful than she was, and so she dressed Snow White in rags and made her cook, scrub, and fetch water from the well, as though she were a servant.

Each day the Queen asked the Spirit of the Magic Mirror, "Magic Mirror on the wall, who is the fairest one of all?"

And each day the Mirror replied, "You are the fairest one of all." But one day the Mirror said, "But hold, a lovely maid I see, alas she is more fair than thee."

"Alas for her!" cried the angry Queen. "Reveal her name."

"Lips red as a rose, hair black as ebony, skin white as snow…."

"Snow White!" gasped the Queen.

Meanwhile, Snow White was in the courtyard scrubbing the steps. As she leaned over the well to get more water, she sang to the doves nearby. She told them that the well was a special wishing well.

Then Snow White peered down the well and made a wish—to find her true love. Suddenly she saw the reflection of a young man. She looked up and saw a handsome prince.

"Oh!" she cried, and ran into the castle.

The Prince had heard the singing and discovered Snow White. He had been searching for the one girl he could love— and he had found her.

"Did I frighten you?" called the young man. "Wait—please don't run away." He began to sing to her.

Snow White crept out on a little balcony to listen, with her heart beating very fast. Her dream had come true! She kissed a dove, which flew down to give her kiss to the stranger.

Snow White didn't know that the Queen had been watching.

When the Queen saw the young man and heard his words of love for Snow White, she was enraged. She decided to get rid of Snow White once and for all.

The Queen called for the Huntsman. "Take her far into the forest… where she can pick wild flowers," she ordered.

"Yes, your majesty," he replied.

"And there…you will kill her!"

"But your majesty, the little princess—" he protested.

"To make doubly sure you do not fail, bring back her heart in this," stormed the cruel Queen, handing him a small box.

The frightened Huntsman took Snow White into the forest, but when the terrible moment came he could not bear to kill her.

"**F**orgive me!" cried the Huntsman, kneeling before the frightened girl. "Run, run away! Hide!" He told the princess that the Queen was mad with jealousy and wanted her dead. "Never come back!" he added.

The terrified Snow White ran deep into the forest. Huge trees seemed to stretch out to grab her. Glowing eyes glared at her from the dark undergrowth. At last, she threw herself on the ground and sobbed bitterly.

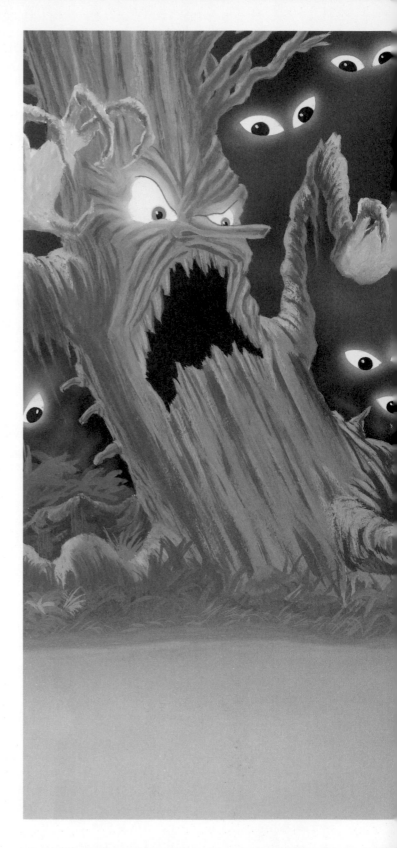

Eventually, Snow White's sobs died away. She looked up to find herself surrounded by squirrels, rabbits, deer, birds, and other forest animals. But when she sat up they scurried away. She began to sing to them, and they circled around her.

Then she asked for their help. "Maybe you know where I can stay," she said to them. The birds twittered to show they did, and soon all the forest folk led her to a tiny house in a clearing.

"It's just like a doll's house!" said Snow White. She peered around the inside. "Seven little chairs…must be seven little children. Seven untidy little children." Snow White thought that if she cleaned the house for them they may let her stay.

Now, the little house belonged to the Seven Dwarfs, who worked in a nearby diamond mine. Every morning they set off for the mine. They worked all day in the deep tunnels, hacking precious stones out of the earth with their pickaxes. The Seven Dwarfs worked hard, but they were a very happy bunch.

Each evening, as the sun was setting, the Seven
Dwarfs stopped work. They locked the new diamonds
away and walked home. They loved to whistle and
sing during their journey. Doc led the way, holding his
lantern, followed by Grumpy, Happy, Sleepy, Sneezy,
Bashful, and Dopey.

Meanwhile, the birds and animals helped Snow White tidy the little house. They swept away the dust and cobwebs, scrubbed the dirty clothes, and washed the dishes. Snow White made a delicious pot of soup. At last, tired out, she went upstairs to the bedroom. There were seven little beds, each with a name.

"Doc, Happy, Sneezy, Dopey, Grumpy, Bashful, and Sleepy. What funny names for children!" said Snow White. "I'm a little sleepy myself." And she fell asleep lying on the little beds.

As the Seven Dwarfs reached their house, they saw the windows all lit up. "Mark my words, there's trouble a-brewing," said Grumpy. They stuck their heads through the door, then tiptoed inside.

"Look," said Doc, "the floor—it's been swept!"

"Our cobwebs are missing!" said Bashful.

"My cup's been washed!"

"Sink's empty!"

"Something's cooking. Smells good!"

"Don't touch it, you fools!" shouted Grumpy.

Doc looked up the stairs. "It's up there," he said. The Seven Dwarfs were very nervous as they climbed the stairs, holding onto one another in fear. They tiptoed into the room just as Snow White yawned and stretched her arms under the sheet.

Doc snatched off the sheet.

But no monster lay there. "Why, it's—it's a girl!" cried Doc.

Snow White woke up with a start. She realized these were no children. "Oh, why, you're little men! How do you do?" She began to name them: Doc, Bashful, Sleepy, Sneezy, Happy, Dopey, and Grumpy.

"We know who we are. Ask her who she is," said Grumpy.

"Who are you, my dear?" asked Doc.

"I'm Snow White."

The Seven Dwarfs gasped. Snow White the princess!

"Please don't send me away," begged Snow White. She told them that the Queen would kill her if she went home. "I'll keep house for you. I'll wash…an' sew…an' sweep…an' cook…."

"Cook?" asked the little men. When they found out she could make gooseberry pie, they cheered.

"Hurray!" shouted the Seven Dwarfs. "She stays!"

Delighted, Snow White ran downstairs to stir the soup. Soon she called, "Supper!"

Meanwhile, the evil Queen hurried to her Magic Mirror. "Magic Mirror on the wall, who now is the fairest one of all?"

The Mirror replied, "Over the seven jeweled hills, beyond the seven falls, in the cottage of the Seven Dwarfs dwells Snow White, fairest one of all."

The Queen told the Spirit of the Magic Mirror that Snow White was dead. She held out the box as proof.

"Snow White still lives," the Mirror replied. "Tis the heart of a pig you hold in your hand!"

The Queen rushed down to her dungeon. She would find Snow White herself. She mixed a magic potion to change herself into an ugly old woman. "Now begin thy magic spell!" she cried, and drank it down.

The Queen's voice turned to a cackle, her hair became white, her elegant hands shrank to claws, and her face became wrinkled and warty.

"Ha, ha!" she screeched. "A perfect disguise!"

She hobbled over to her book of magic spells to choose a curse. "Ah! A poison apple! Sleeping death!" she cackled.

"But wait—there may be an antidote. Nothing must be overlooked. Ah! Here it is," she cried. "The victim of the sleeping death can only be revived by love's first kiss. Love's first kiss? Bah! No fear of that!"

The old crone dipped an apple into the poisoned brew. She pulled out the gleaming red fruit and tucked it into a basket.

In the cottage, Snow White and the Seven Dwarfs were having a celebration. Happy sang a song while the other Dwarfs played all sorts of instruments. Dopey stood on Sneezy's shoulders so he would be tall enough to dance with Snow White. All was going well until Sneezy felt his nose start to twitch. "A-a-a-ah-TCHOOO!"

The next morning, the Seven Dwarfs left for work. "Now don't forgit, my dear, the old Queen's a sly one," they said, "so beware of strangers."

"I'll be all right," said Snow White cheerfully. And she kissed Dopey and all the others on the head as they left.

The wicked Queen hurried through the forest and stopped when she reached the edge of the clearing. She could hear Snow White's lovely voice as she sang inside the cottage while she worked.

"Aha!" said the Queen. "The little men will be away and she'll be alone...."

The Queen went up to the cottage window and saw Snow White working in the kitchen. "Making pies?" croaked the old woman. "Like to try my apples?" And she held out the poisoned apple.

Snow White was surprised and a little afraid. The birds realized the danger and flew at the old woman, trying to drive her away.

"Shoo! Shoo!" cried Snow White, rushing out of the house. "What do you mean by attacking a poor old lady?" She led the old woman inside and made her sit down.

The birds and animals watched in horror. "We must warn the Dwarfs in the mine!" they chirped and chattered to each other. Off they went, flying and running as fast as they could.

The Witch held up the shiny red fruit. "I'll share a secret with you," she said. "It's a magic wishing apple."

"A wishing apple?"

"One bite, and all your dreams will come true. Now make a wish…and take a bite."

Snow White took the apple, closed her eyes, wished that her Prince would find her, and took a big bite.

By this time the animals had reached the mine. They pecked and pushed at the Seven Dwarfs, but the little men couldn't understand what was wrong. At last, Sleepy said, "Maybe the old Queen's got Snow White!"

"Oh, I feel strange!" gasped Snow White, back at the cottage. The wicked Queen watched eagerly. Snow White took one deep breath, then fell to the floor. The poisoned apple rolled away.

"Ha, ha!" croaked the old woman. "Her breath will still—her blood congeal. Now I'll be the fairest in the land."

The Seven Dwarfs arrived at the clearing just as the hag disappeared into the forest.

The Seven Dwarfs dashed after the Queen. Lightning flashed and rain poured down. The Queen began to climb a rocky mountain. "There she goes! After her!" cried Grumpy.

The Queen scrambled higher and higher. At last she reached the edge of a cliff and could go no farther. "I'll crush your bones!" she shrieked. Grabbing a dead branch, she tried to push a huge boulder down on the Seven Dwarfs.

Suddenly a bolt of lightning hit the ledge. It broke off and fell down…down…into the valley below, taking the Queen to her death.

The Seven Dwarfs returned to the cottage to find Snow White lying on the floor, seemingly dead. She looked so beautiful that they didn't have the heart to bury her. Instead, they built her a golden coffin and placed it in the woods. Each day they brought flowers, and the forest creatures visited her.

In time, people heard of the beautiful maiden lying in the woods. The Prince also heard about the maiden. He decided to take a look for himself.

As soon as the Prince reached the coffin in the clearing, he knew she was the lovely girl of the wishing well. Heartbroken, he bent over and kissed Snow White, then bowed his head in silence.

Suddenly, Snow White's eyelids fluttered open. She yawned, sat up, and was amazed to find herself looking into the eyes of her beloved prince. He joyfully gathered her in his arms. The Seven Dwarfs danced up and down, and all the little forest animals chirped and chattered with delight.

Snow White kissed each of the Seven Dwarfs goodbye. The Prince lifted her onto his white horse, and led the way to his castle. There they were married, and, of course, lived happily ever after.

Walt Disney's ROBIN HOOD

Robin Hood lived with his Merry Men in Sherwood Forest. Some people said he was a hero. Others called him a bandit. Why? Because he robbed from the rich to give to the poor.

One day Robin and his friend Little John saw King Richard's golden carriage pass by. But the king was away at war. Instead, it was the king's wicked brother, Prince John, pretending to be king.

Seeing him there gave Robin an idea.

Robin and Little John disguised themselves as lady fortune-tellers. Then they raced after the royal coach.

Robin cried, "Fortunes forecast, lucky charms!"

Inside the coach, Prince John had grown bored with counting his money. He was even more bored with Sir Hiss, the snake who served as his aide.

Sir Hiss spent his life trying to please the prince, but always managed to irritate him instead. Today, Sir Hiss had accidentally mentioned King Richard.

"Silly serpent!" Prince John snarled. "I told you never to mention my brother's name." Just then, Prince John saw the fortune-tellers and was ready for some amusement. Sir Hiss tried to warn him that the female fortune-tellers may be bandits. "You've hissed your last hisss…suspicious snake," Prince John scolded as he locked Sir Hiss in his basket.

Prince John ordered his coachmen to halt. "Step inside," he said to Robin and Little John.

Robin and Little John set up their crystal ball and put on a fine show for the prince. They knew exactly how to appeal to his greed.

Prince John gazed into the crystal ball, so charmed by the thought of riches that he paid no attention to the hissing sounds coming from the serpent's basket. Sir Hiss suspected a trick.

Sir Hiss hissed even louder when Robin grabbed hold of Sir John's huge sacks of gold and slid them quietly across the floor. The snake poked his long tail through a crack in the basket and tried to hang onto the gold, but he failed.

Robin leaped from the carriage with the gold, pausing only long enough to snatch the fancy ermine cloak right off Prince John's back.

Meanwhile, Little John managed to drain even more coins from a locked trunk, stealing them from right under the noses of the bearers who were supposed to be guarding them.

Then Little John loosened the wheels on the golden carriage.

When the prince finally realized that he had been tricked, he was enraged. "I've been robbed!" yelled the furious prince.

Robin Hood and Little John were already running away. Prince John ordered his guards to follow the thieves, but the carriage didn't get very far before its wheels fell off.

With his carriage disabled, Prince John had no hope of catching up with the thieves.

He had to watch helplessly, dressed only in his underwear, as Robin and Little John disappeared into Sherwood Forest, both of them loaded with jingling coins and jewels.

By the time Prince John returned to his castle, he was beside himself with rage.

He sent for his henchman, the wicked Sheriff of Nottingham. It was the Sheriff's job to collect taxes, and he was very good at it. He could sniff out gold wherever it was hidden.

For example, a poor blacksmith had tried to hide a few coins inside the cast on his broken leg, but the Sheriff simply grabbed the blacksmith's leg and shook out the gold. Even the good Friar Tuck couldn't stop him.

So when Prince John decided to take his revenge on Robin by raising the taxes yet again, the Sheriff was more than happy to help.

He headed for Skippy Bunny's house.

It was Skippy's birthday, and his sisters had saved all year to give him a shiny new gold coin.

"Happy birthday," the Sheriff said. With that, he snatched the coin, and was gone, leaving Skippy in tears.

Fortunately, Robin Hood showed up a few minutes later. Skippy stopped crying when he saw that Robin had brought not only more gold, but some special birthday gifts—a bow and arrows!

Absolutely everyone was excited about the Tournament of Golden Arrows. The best archer in the Kingdom would win a kiss from the lovely Maid Marian.

Robin loved Marian, even though he was afraid "such a high born lady of quality" would never marry an outlaw.

He decided to enter the tournament disguised as a stork. With luck, he would win Marian's kiss, and Prince John would never be the wiser.

Robin didn't know that Prince John had devised the tournament as a trap. Everyone knew that Robin Hood was the best archer in the land.

By the end of the day, only two archers were left—the stork and the Sheriff.

Then the stork fired his final arrow... a perfect bull's-eye!

Maid Marian was overjoyed, for she knew the stork must be none other than Robin Hood himself. And although Robin didn't know it, she was in love with him, too.

"Archer, I commend you, and because of your superior skill, you shall get what is coming to you," Prince John said. Then, as Robin bowed, Prince John sliced off the stork disguise with a swipe of his sword. "Seize him!" Prince John shouted.

The Sheriff led Robin away.

Robin knew that justice would only be done when King Richard returned. And so he said bravely, "Long live King Richard!"

Mention of the King's name made Prince John leap angrily from his throne. Then he felt someone holding a dagger to his back. It was Little John, disguised as a fat duke.

"Tell him to untie my buddy or I'll..." Little John said to him.

The prince had no choice. Robin and Little John had bested him again.

But the two outlaws still had to fight a messy battle with the guards before they made their escape back to Sherwood Forest. Robin Hood waved to his Maid Marian as he disappeared into the woods.

Back at the castle, Prince John was furious. And as usual, he was taking it out on Sir Hiss. This time he squeezed the snake until he turned green.

"Double the taxes," said the prince. "Triple the taxes! Squeeze every last drop out of those insolent...peasants."

So the prince raised taxes, and the Sheriff happily set out on his mission to make the poor people of Nottingham even poorer. Finally there was only one coin left in town—in the church collection box. The Sheriff took it.

"You thievin' scoundrel!" shouted Friar Tuck. He was so angry, he flew at the Sheriff with fists raised. That gave the Sheriff the excuse he had been waiting for. He threw the good Friar in prison.

At long last, Prince John was sure he had the perfect trap for Robin Hood. He was so excited that he pounded his fist on the table, frightening Sir Hiss.

"I'll use that fat Friar as bait to trap Robin Hood," said the prince. "When our elusive hero tries to rescue the corpulent cleric...my men will be ready."

Sir Hiss shook in fright.

News traveled fast, and it was not long before Robin heard about Friar Tuck's imprisonment. So he put on a new disguise and headed with Little John for Prince John's castle.

"Who goes there?" a guard called.

"Alms for the poor," Robin cried, dressed as a poor blind man. The guard was convinced Robin was a simple beggar, and let him pass.

Robin whipped off his beggar's disguise and dressed up like a guard. Then he and Little John crept into the castle to find the Sheriff.

The Sheriff was supposed to be on guard duty, but Robin found him sound asleep outside the cell door. Robin stretched out his hand for the keys, but the sound of footsteps made him dart back into the shadows.

Two guards marched past. Little John jumped the guards from behind, and soon had them trussed up like holiday turkeys.

Meanwhile, Robin grabbed the keys, and tossed them to his friend. "Now, you release Friar Tuck and the others, and I'll drop in on the royal treasury," he said.

Little John found the cell full of citizens who could not pay their taxes. Even the Bunny family was in chains. But no one was happier to see Little John than Friar Tuck.

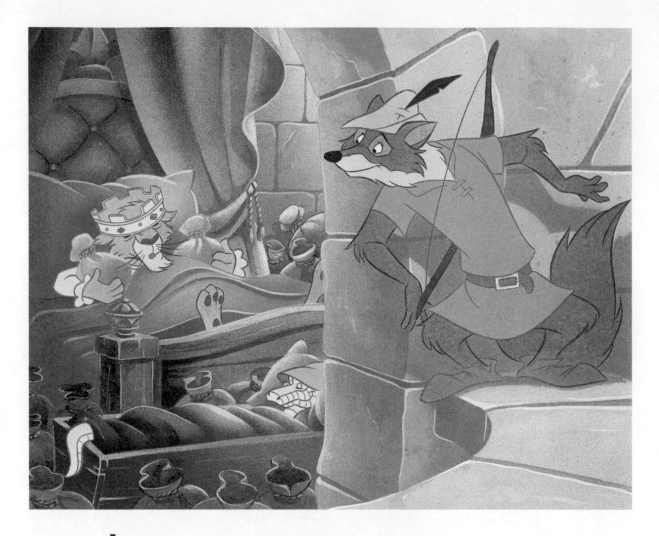

In the royal bedchamber, all was quiet. Prince John was asleep, with his crown askew on his head. He was tightly clutching two bags of gold, dreaming of the day when all the money in the world would be his. More bags of gold were heaped around his bed and all around the room.

Sir Hiss was sound asleep in his cradle, his sharp eyes squeezed shut. Neither of them stirred as Robin crept silently into the room.

Watching them sleep, Robin Hood worked out a clever plan.

Carefully, Robin tied a long rope to the end of an arrow. Then he fired the arrow out the window, to the exact spot where he knew Little John, Friar Tuck, and the rest of his friends were waiting.

Very quietly, he attached Prince John's bags of gold to the rope, one by one, and slid them to his waiting friends.

As quickly as the bags of gold rolled in, Little John and Friar Tuck untied them from the rope while the freed prisoners waited anxiously.

Robin was quietly loading the last bags of gold right from under Prince John's nose when some tiny sound caused Sir Hiss's eyes to flash open.

Robin Hood barely had time to grab onto the rope himself, before Prince John and Sir Hiss flew into action. "They're getting away with my gold!" shouted Prince John.

But try as they might, Prince John and Sir Hiss could not reach Robin.

With his tail wrapped around Prince John's ankle and Prince John just barely holding on to his bed, Hiss stretched as far as he could. He managed to grab hold of the last sack of gold with his fangs. But the sack ripped, and the gold coins fell tumbling to the ground, to Prince John's horror.

Still, Prince John's cries woke the palace archers. They shot their arrows at Robin as Little John pulled his friend to safety.

Robin slid down the rope and into Little John's arms. But the friends were still in danger. The Sheriff was finally awake, and had called the guards into action.

"Keep going! Don't worry about me!" Robin said. He stayed behind to confront the Sheriff.

The Friar, Little John, and the freed prisoners ran for the palace drawbridge with the gold.

Meanwhile, Robin Hood climbed the walls of the castle tower, the wicked Sheriff and his band of archers hot on his heels.

"We got him now!" roared the evil Sheriff.

Then the Sheriff tripped and the fire from his torch touched the drapes, causing a fire!

The flames from the drapes spread throughout the castle. After a chase through the castle, Robin leapt from the tower into the moat just in time! He swam across the moat under a hail of arrows, and managed to escape into Sherwood Forest.

Meanwhile, Little John loaded the freed prisoners and the gold into a cart and sped across the castle drawbridge to safety.

Prince John's castle and his dreams were both in flames, and his fortune had been stolen. The only one upon whom he could exercise his fury was…Sir Hiss.

There was great joy in Sherwood Forest that night. Everyone cheered loudly for Robin Hood, even little Skippy Bunny.

A few days later, all the bells in the country rang to announce the return of King Richard. He would soon bring justice to the land!

Friar Tuck went to ask King Richard a very important question. Could Robin Hood marry the king's niece, the lovely Maid Marian?

"What?!!" King Richard cried. He wasn't sure at first, but then he accepted. "It appears that I now have an outlaw for an in-law. Not bad."

So shortly after that, Maid Marian's secret wish finally came true. She married her beloved Robin Hood, and they lived happily ever after.

And all of Nottingham celebrated with the happy couple at the wedding.

Walt Disney's Cinderella

Once upon a time, in a faraway kingdom, there lived a young girl called Cinderella. She lived in a mansion with her Stepmother and two Stepsisters, Anastasia and Drizella.

Cinderella was kind and lovely, while her stepsisters were selfish and ugly. Her Stepmother did not like Cinderella. She made her do all the housework and sleep in the attic.

But Cinderella always looked on the sunny side of life. She did her work cheerfully and made friends with the mice and birds for company.

Now, the King of the country was hoping his son would marry and settle down. But how could he get his son to meet the right girl? Then he had a wonderful idea: He would have a ball in honor of his son. "And if all the eligible maidens in my kingdom just happened to be there…"

And so one morning the palace messenger appeared at the door of Cinderella's house with a special invitation.

"**A** ball! In honor of his highness the Prince…and, by royal command, every eligible maiden is to attend!" said the Stepmother as she read the invitation.

"Why, that means I can go, too," said Cinderella.

"Ha! Ha!" screeched the stepsisters. Then they began to mimic Cinderella at the ball. "I'd be honored, your highness…would you mind holding my broom?"

"Why not? After all, I'm still a member of the family," said Cinderella firmly.

"**W**ell, I see no reason why you can't go, if you get all your work done," said the Stepmother.

Cinderella's stepsisters were very upset. "Mother, do you realize what you just said?" they cried.

"Of course. I said *if*," the Stepmother replied slyly.

"Oh, *if*!" said the stepsisters, grinning at each other.

And of course, Cinderella would have to find a suitable dress to wear to the ball. She hurried up to the attic to see what she could find.

In her room, Cinderella opened an old trunk and lifted out a dress with puffed sleeves. The mice watched her curiously. "Isn't it lovely?" she asked, looking in the mirror. "It was my mother's."

"Ess…butta…butta…dessa old," said a thin little mouse called Jaq.

"Oh, I'll fix that," said Cinderella. "I'll need a sash…a ruffle…"

Then the stepsisters called, "Cinderella!"

"Poor Cinderelly!" said the mice. "Every time she finds a minute…that's the time when they begin it."

"Oh, well…guess my dress'll have to wait," Cinderella said. Then she called down to her stepsisters, "All right, I'm coming!" She hurried out of the attic.

"You'll see!" squeaked Jaq. "They'll fix her. She'll never get her dress done."

Cinderella found her stepmother in the front hall with Anastasia and Drizella. They told her to wash the hall floor, even though she had cleaned it the day before.

"When you're through, and before you begin your regular chores, I have a few little things…" said the Stepmother.

Anastasia and Drizella also found some extra work for Cinderella to do. They wanted her to iron their ball gowns and curl their hair for the party—that is, after sweeping the fireplace, shining the pots and pans, and doing the laundry.

Cinderella had no choice but to do as they asked. All day long she worked, thinking sadly of her dress in the attic.

Meanwhile the mice and birds worked on Cinderella's dress.

Jaq and his new friend Gus scampered down to the stepsisters' room to see what they could find. The sisters were going through their cupboard.

"These old rags," sniffed Anastasia, dropping a sash on the floor.

Then Drizella tossed some beads she was tired of into a corner.

Gus and Jaq dragged the sash and beads up to the attic, right past Lucifer, the cat. When the other mice saw what Gus and Jaq had found, they cheered.

At the end of the day, Cinderella was still working with the stepsisters. Drizella made Cinderella help her try on one dress after another. None of them could make her look as pretty as Cinderella.

At last the sisters paraded downstairs, very pleased with themselves.

"I'm not going," sighed Cinderella as she climbed slowly to her attic. "Oh, well—what's a royal ball?" But when she opened the door her eyes lit up like stars.

"**S**urprise!" cried the mice and the birds. They couldn't wait to see her dressed in the pretty gown, and they were especially proud of all their work.

"Why, I never dreamed…it's such a surprise!" gasped Cinderella. "How can I ever…why…oh, thank you so much!" She could hardly believe that she would be able to go to the Prince's ball after all! She took off her old clothes and slipped into her new dress. She twirled around in front of the mirror. As she hurried out the door she blew a kiss to her little friends.

Downstairs, Drizella and Anastasia were being given a last minute check by their mother. The carriage was waiting for them outside.

The Stepmother was saying, "Now remember, when you are presented to his highness, be sure to—" She stopped and gasped. She couldn't believe her eyes. There, coming down the grand staircase, was Cinderella, prettier than ever and wearing a charming dress!

"Please! Wait for me!" called Cinderella. She ran down the stairs and held out her skirt. "Isn't it lovely? Do you like it? Do you?" she asked.

Drizella and Anastasia stared for a moment, horrified. "Mother, no!" they babbled, both talking at once. "She can't go! Do something!"

"Girls, girls!" said the Stepmother, waving her hand for silence. "After all, we did make a bargain." She turned to Cinderella. "Didn't we?"

Her eyes narrowed as she looked at Cinderella. "My, how very clever…these beads—they give it just the right touch, don't you think so, Drizella?"

"No, they do not!" screeched Drizella. "They…they…why, you little thief. Those are my beads. Give them here!" She snatched the beads from Cinderella's neck.

"Look! That's my sash! She's wearing my sash!" yelled Anastasia, ripping off the sash the mice had sewn on so carefully.

"No, stop!" wailed Cinderella, trying to defend herself. But Drizella and Anastasia tore at her dress, pulling off all of the frills and all of the bows. Soon Cinderella's beautiful gown was in tatters. It looked worse than her ordinary work clothes.

"Girls! That's quite enough," called the Stepmother curtly. "Hurry along now…both of you." And the three of them sailed through the great front door to the waiting carriage, leaving Cinderella alone and miserable in the hall.

Cinderella rushed into the garden and knelt by a stone bench, sobbing her heart out. It was so unfair! She'd always had faith in her dreams. And it had been her dearest wish to go to the ball, to wear a pretty dress, and to dance like other young girls!

"I can't believe, not anymore…there's nothing left to believe in," Cinderella moaned.

The mice watched miserably. Jaq and Gus knew that Cinderella's stepsisters didn't want her to go to the ball, but they could hardly believe that anyone could be so mean.

All the animals felt sad. Major, the old cart horse, and Bruno, the dog, tried to comfort Cinderella.

But something strange was twinkling in the air! Very soon, a kind-faced little lady was sitting on the bench, patting Cinderella's head and saying, "You can't go to the ball looking like that! But we'll have to hurry...."

"Why...then you must be—" said Cinderella.

"Your Fairy Godmother, of course!" said the stranger with a kindly smile.

N ow let's see...," said the Fairy Godmother. With a few waves of her wand, she began making magic! She found a pumpkin for a coach and turned Cinderella's mice friends into horses. The horse, Major, became the Coachman, and Bruno, the family dog, turned into a Footman!

"**W**ell, hop in, my dear; we can't waste time."

"But…" Cinderella looked at her tatters.

"Now don't try to thank me…," said the Fairy Godmother.

"I mean, I do, but…don't you think my dress.…"

"Yes, yes, my dear, it's lovely—" Suddenly the Fairy Godmother's eyes opened wide. "Heavens, child, you can't go in that!"

The Fairy Godmother measured Cinderella with her wand. "What a gown this will be! Bibbidi, bobbidi, boo!" A shower of starlight whirled around Cinderella. As it melted away, there she stood in a sparkling ball gown.

"Oh!" gasped Cinderella, twirling around. "Did you ever see such a beautiful dress? And glass slippers! It's like a dream!"

"But like all dreams…well, I'm afraid this can't last forever. You'll have only till midnight and then…the spell will be broken.…"

"It's more than I ever hoped for!" said Cinderella, kissing the Fairy Godmother.

Away went Cinderella in her enchanted coach, racing beneath the starry sky toward the palace. Hundreds of people were gathered there for the ball. All the eligible maidens were being presented to the Prince. He didn't look very happy at all.

In the balcony above, the King and the Grand Duke watched. The King was feeling very grumpy. "Oh…the boy isn't cooperating," he growled.

"If I may say so, your majesty, I did try to warn you…," said the Grand Duke nervously.

"There must be at least one who'd make a suitable wife!" said the King.

Just then Drizella and Anastasia were being presented. The Prince rolled his eyes when he saw them. "I give up!" muttered the King.

But something had caught the Prince's eye. A beautiful young woman was wandering in the hall just outside the ballroom. She was by far the loveliest maiden at the palace that evening. Without so much as an "Excuse me," he strode out of the ballroom and went up to Cinderella.

The Prince bowed to her and without a word they walked slowly into the ballroom and began to dance.

The King was beside himself with joy. "Look at that!" he hissed, poking the Grand Duke. "Who is she?"

"I've never seen her before, sire," said the puzzled Grand Duke.

"Well, find out!" ordered the King.

Cinderella and the Prince waltzed 'round and 'round. They had eyes only for each other. Cinderella was sure that she was in love, as she gazed at her handsome partner.

All the guests were mystified. "Do we know her?" Drizella asked her sister.

"Well the Prince certainly seems to!" said Anastasia.

The Stepmother watched as the couple waltzed away towards the palace balcony. "There is something familiar about her," she said.

Cinderella and the Prince strolled into the palace garden and danced beneath the stars. But just as the Prince bent to kiss her, the palace clock began to chime midnight!

"I must go!" said Cinderella.

"Why?" replied the puzzled Prince. But Cinderella was already dashing away.

"Wait! I don't even know your name!" cried the Prince desperately.

But Cinderella didn't answer as she ran down the great staircase to her coach. She was in such a hurry that she left one of her glass slippers behind.

The Prince took the slipper to the Grand Duke. It was his only clue to finding the maiden with whom he had fallen in love.

To find its owner, the Grand Duke issued a proclamation that every maiden in the kingdom would try on the slipper.

Meanwhile Cinderella's coach was racing home. Ding! chimed the clock. Ding! Ding! As it reached the twelfth chime, the beautiful coach disappeared. Cinderella was left sitting on a pumpkin beside Major, Bruno, and the four mice.

"I forgot about everything, even the time," sighed Cinderella. "But it was so wonderful, and he was so handsome.... Oh, I'm sure that even the Prince himself couldn't have been more—"

"Your flipper, Cinderelly, your flipper!" squeaked Jaq.

There, on Cinderella's foot, twinkled the other slipper!

All night long the Grand Duke went from house to house, trying the glass slipper on all the sleepy maidens. The news of the search reached Cinderella's house. That's when Cinderella finally realized that her dance partner had been the Prince!

The Stepmother noticed Cinderella's dreamy expression and became very suspicious. She heard her humming music from the ball.

Cinderella raced up to her room to brush her hair. The Stepmother followed her. Before Cinderella could stop her, the wicked woman had locked the door!

Jaq and Gus watched in horror. "We've gotta get that key," whispered Jaq.

Meanwhile, the Grand Duke's coach rumbled into the courtyard. "Mother, Mother, the Grand Duke is here!" screeched Drizella and Anastasia, who had been watching at the window.

The Grand Duke walked slowly up the front stairs. A Footman carried the glass slipper on a velvet pillow.

"You honor our humble home," said the Stepmother. The stepsisters curtsied and giggled.

Anastasia and Drizella elbowed each other out of the way, each wanting to be the first to try on the glass slipper. Each sister tried to get her foot into the slipper. They pushed and squeezed as hard as they could, but it was no use.

Meanwhile, Jaq and Gus had scurried down to the drawing room where the Stepmother was busy talking to the Grand Duke. The brave little mice managed to steal the key from her pocket and had soon dragged it upstairs to Cinderella's attic to free her.

"You are the only ladies of the household, I presume…?" asked the weary Grand Duke.

"There's no one else," replied the Stepmother.

"Very well," said the Grand Duke, walking towards the door. "Good day, madam."

Suddenly he heard a sweet voice calling, "Please wait! May I try it on?" There on the staircase was Cinderella in her work clothes. The Grand Duke took one look at her feet and smiled. "Come, my child," he said, leading her to a chair. But the angry stepmother tripped the Footman as he carried over the slipper, and it smashed to pieces.

"Oh, no!" wailed the Grand Duke.

"But perhaps this would help," said Cinderella, taking a glass slipper from her pocket. "I have the other slipper."

As the mice cheered and the horrified sisters looked on, the Grand Duke put the slipper on Cinderella's foot. It was a perfect fit!

How happy the Grand Duke was! The King jumped for joy when he heard the news. And as for the Prince—well, in no time at all he married his lovely Cinderella, and they lived happily ever after!

One day Kala the gorilla was walking through the jungle when she heard a strange noise. It was the sound of a baby crying, and it was coming from a house built high up in a tree. Kala crept up to the house.

Inside she found a big mess. In the corner, there was a blue blanket, which moved as she approached it.

Kala pulled back the blanket, and there was the baby. As soon as it saw her, it stopped crying and looked up at her with curious eyes. Then it giggled at her, but Kala still wasn't sure if it was safe to touch. She picked it up by one leg, then with one finger hooked into its diaper.

The baby gurgled and babbled. Then she cradled it in her arms. The baby cooed and snuggled closer. That was when she knew that she would have to keep it. After all, its parents were missing.

Just then, Sabor the leopard appeared! All at once, Kala realized what had happened to the baby's parents, and she knew she had to act fast—the leopard was still hungry.

Sabor growled ferociously and then began to chase Kala. Although she dropped the baby once, Kala managed to keep it away from Sabor and ran to safety with it.

Kala took the baby to the other gorillas.

"It's freaky-looking," said a gorilla baby named Terk, when Kala showed her the child.

"He's a baby," Kala explained to Terk. "I'm going to be his mother now."

But Kerchak, the leader of the gorillas, was not pleased. "I cannot let you put our family in danger," he said.

"Does he look dangerous to you?" Kala asked him.

Kerchak roared in frustration, but finally he agreed to let Kala keep the baby. Kala named the baby Tarzan.

Kala took care of Tarzan and raised him as her own son. She knew that he was not like the other babies, but he was hers, and that was what mattered. She taught him everything he needed to know about life in the jungle, and she treated him like a member of her family, even though Kerchak would not accept Tarzan as his son.

Tarzan soon learned that he was different. He wanted to be one of the gang, but he never seemed to fit in. One day Terk told him that the other gorillas would play with him if he got an elephant hair. Tarzan took a flying leap into the water where the elephants swam and yanked the tail of an elephant. The elephant panicked, and there was a stampede. Tarzan and the apes survived, but Kerchack was furious that Tarzan had put the apes in such danger.

"He's only a child," Kala said.

"Look at him," said Kerchak. "He will never be one of us."

Tarzan was very upset as he looked at his reflection in the water. He thought that if he put mud on his face he might look more like the other gorillas.

"Why am I so different?" he asked his mother. "Look at me!"

"I am, Tarzan," Kala answered. "And do you know what I see? I see two eyes like mine, and a nose…somewhere…ah here. Two ears…And let's see, what else?"

"Two hands?" said Tarzan, holding his hands up to his mother's. But he could see how different they were. He looked down.

"Close your eyes," Kala said as she put Tarzan's hand to his heart. "What do you feel?"

"My heart."

Kala hugged Tarzan close to her so that he could hear her heartbeat.

"See?" she said. "We're exactly the same. Kerchak just can't see that."

"I'll make him see it!" Tarzan said. "I'll be the best ape ever!"

Tarzan grew up to be an ape like no other. He could swing on vines with ease, slide along the mossy branches, even climb up waterfalls. He was at home in the jungle. And Terk became his best friend.

One day, Tarzan and Terk were wrestling. They were having so much fun they didn't notice that someone was stalking them.

The stalker was Sabor, the ferocious leopard that had killed Tarzan's parents. This time she was after Tarzan and his gorilla family. Though Terk and Tarzan didn't see her, luckily someone else did. Just as Sabor was about to attack, Tarzan leaped out of the way. Moments later, Kerchak rushed in to help his family.

Kerchak grabbed Sabor by the tail and tried to swing her around. But the leopard was fast and very strong. She lashed out, throwing Kerchak to the ground. When Tarzan saw what was happening, he leaped to help Kerchak, spear in hand.

All of his years in the jungle had taught Tarzan well. He was an expert hunter.

Tarzan crept around the leopard with his spear ready.

But when Sabor lunged at him, the spear broke. As they wrestled, the tip of the spear fell off a cliff. Tarzan jumped down to retrieve it, and the leopard followed. They fell into dense foliage and the gorillas could not see either of them. For a while there was nothing but an eerie silence.

Then Tarzan emerged, holding the limp leopard over his head. The other gorillas screamed in delight. Tarzan knelt before his leader. He presented the leopard to Kerchak to honor him. But before the ape could respond, they heard a loud bang. There had never been such a sound in their jungle before.

Kerchak ordered his family to go deeper into the jungle where they would be safe, but Tarzan lingered behind. He was curious about the strange sound he had heard, and he wanted to know where it had come from. He found a shotgun shell and smelled the gunpowder inside. Soon Tarzan heard strange, new voices.

Tarzan watched as three humans approached: Professor Porter, his daughter, Jane, and their guide, Clayton. Jane and her father were excited to be standing in a gorilla nest. Porter explained that gorillas nested in family groups.

Clayton scoffed, "These are wild beasts that would sooner tear your head off than look at you."

Just then, Clayton thought he heard a noise. He shot his rifle right up into the air, narrowly missing Tarzan, who was hiding in the trees above. Clayton and Professor Porter moved on to set up camp, but Jane stayed behind. She wanted to sketch an adorable baby baboon.

But then the baboon stole her sketchbook and started tearing the pages out. When she took them back, the baby started to cry. Suddenly, Jane found herself surrounded by snarling baboons.

Just as the baboons were about to attack Jane, Tarzan lifted her away from them. He flew through the air with Jane in his arms, swinging on vines and sliding along mossy branches with Jane hanging on for dear life.

When they were finally safe from the baboons, Jane had lost only one boot and her parasol. Tarzan was very curious about this creature who seemed very much like him. First, he sniffed her bare foot. But Jane was ticklish.

"Get off!" she cried, giggling and then kicking at him.

Then he took off one of Jane's gloves and compared her hand to his. They looked the same, so he listened to her heart to see if that was the same as well. It was! He pulled her head to his chest, so that she could listen to his.

"Thank you. That's a lovely heartbeat," she said, backing away.

Tarzan thumped his chest with a fist saying, "Tarzan."

Jane pointed to herself and said, "Jane."

Tarzan could hardly believe it. He had finally found somebody just like him!

Meanwhile, Terk, some of her ape pals, and Tantor, the elephant, had found the humans' camp. They were having a lot of fun with all the strange things they found there. They were also making a big mess.

When Tarzan led Jane back to the camp, she was delighted to see gorillas for the first time. But then Kerchak arrived and roared at Jane. The gorillas left very quickly, and Tarzan went with them. Soon Jane's father and Clayton returned. They were glad that she had made it to the camp safely, but they had a hard time believing her story about the "Ape Man."

Back in the gorilla nest, Kerchak told his family to stay away from the strangers.

But Tarzan confronted Kerchak. "Why does anyone different threaten you?" he asked.

Meanwhile, after describing Tarzan and sketching him, Jane tried to convince her father to meet Tarzan. "Think of what we could learn from him," she said.

"Professor, you are here to find gorillas," said Clayton, "not indulge some girlish fantasy."

"I didn't imagine him!" Jane replied. "Tarzan is real."

As she spoke the words, Tarzan dropped out of the trees right in front of her, as if to prove her point.

Jane saw the ape man as an empty slate to fill with knowledge. She decided to teach Tarzan about the world she knew. She showed him slides of people and places he had never seen. She taught him how to speak English and even how to read.

Jane was a good teacher, and Tarzan quickly learned what he had missed growing up in the jungle. The more Tarzan learned about Jane and her world, the more he wanted to know. And the more he knew about Jane and her world, the more he liked her.

Tarzan taught Jane about his world, the jungle. He took her to the most beautiful spots so that she could sketch. They went to the part of the jungle where the parrots lived. The colorful birds perched on both of them, and Jane sketched them.

He even taught Jane how to swing on a vine, though she was a little scared at first. Soon she was swinging through the jungle with her new friend. They were both so happy that they thought their happiness could never end.

Tarzan wanted to show Jane how much he cared about her. One of the slides Tarzan had seen showed a man giving a lady flowers. That gave Tarzan an idea.

Tarzan brought Jane flowers, but when he arrived, the camp was being packed up. Jane and her father were going home to England. They wanted Tarzan to come with them. Jane explained that if Tarzan went with them, he could never come back.

"Jane must stay with Tarzan," Tarzan said, offering her the flowers.

"I can't," said Jane before she ran away in tears.

Clayton told Tarzan that if Jane saw gorillas, she would stay. Tarzan finally agreed to lead them to the gorillas.

Tarzan told Terk and Tantor to distract Kerchak. Terk dressed up in one of Jane's dresses, and Tantor's trunk was dressed like the professor. While Kerchak chased them through the woods, Tarzan brought Jane, Clayton, and Professor Porter to the gorilla nest.

Jane had a wonderful time playing with the baby gorillas while Clayton was busy writing something down.

Later, Tarzan taught Jane to speak gorilla.

"Ou-ou-ee-eh-ooo," she repeated after him.

The baby gorillas all started to chatter, jumping around her excitedly.

"What did I say?" Jane asked.

"Jane stay with Tarzan," he said.

Just then, Terk and Tantor burst in, frantically running away from Kerchak. Kerchak appeared as well and realized that he had been tricked. He saw Clayton's gun and went wild with rage, roaring and trying to attack. Tarzan wrestled him to the ground and struggled to hold him there.

"Go! Now!" Tarzan cried to his human friends.

When they were gone, he realized what he had done and hung his head in shame.

"I asked you to protect our family and you betrayed us all," Kerchak said.

Tarzan climbed up into a tall tree to be alone. He looked out over the jungle and at the boat that was about to take Jane away. Kala approached him.

"I'm so confused," he said. He didn't know what was right anymore, or even who he was.

"Come with me," Kala said. "There's something I should have shown you long ago."

Kala took Tarzan to the tree house where she had found him so many years before. There, she showed him a picture of his parents.

"Now you know. Tarzan, I just want you to be happy," she said, as Tarzan looked at the picture. "Whatever you decide."

Tarzan was torn between his ape family and his new human friends. Should he stay in the jungle, or go with Jane?

Tarzan put on his father's clothes. He had made his decision.

"No matter where I go," he said to Kala, "you will always be my mother."

"And you will always be in my heart," she replied.

Tears welled up in Kala's eyes as she watched Tarzan walk away upright, in the direction of the boat.

Terk and Tantor hurried to the beach to say goodbye to Tarzan as soon as they heard, but they just missed him as he rowed out to the boat.

Jane was thrilled to see that Tarzan had changed his mind. She told him about all the places they would go together and all the things they would do.

As Tarzan climbed up the ladder to the boat, he couldn't help looking back longingly at the jungle that had been his home for his whole life.

As soon as Tarzan stepped onto the boat, a group of sailors surrounded him, trying to capture him. He got away and climbed way up the mast, but then he fell, hurting his arm. Clayton appeared, and pretended not to recognize him as the sailors grabbed Jane and Professor Porter.

"Sorry about the rude welcome, old boy," he said to Tarzan, "but I couldn't have you making a scene when we put your furry friends in their cages."

But Tarzan didn't understand why Clayton would want to cage the gorillas. "Why?" he asked.

"Why? For 300 pounds sterling a head," Clayton said. "Couldn't have done it without you."

As the sailors dragged him away, along with Jane and Professor Porter, Tarzan let out a howl of pain.

Back in the jungle, Tantor and Terk heard his cry.

"That sounded like Tarzan," Tantor said.

"Yeah, well, why doesn't he get his new friends to help him," said Terk, feeling rejected. "I don't care."

But Tantor said, "Tarzan needs us and we're going to help him! Now pipe down and hang on tight. We've got a boat to catch."

Tantor, in a sudden burst of courage, ran through the jungle with Terk hanging on for dear life. Then, with a huge splash, the elephant belly-flopped into the ocean and swam for the boat.

Once they reached the boat, Terk and Tantor soon freed Tarzan and his friends.

Meanwhile, in the jungle, Clayton found the gorilla nest using the map he made when he had visited it with Tarzan. Then he and his men captured the gorillas in nets. He put some into cages to bring them back to the boat.

The gorillas were scared. They didn't understand what was happening. When Kala was put into a cage, she wished that Tarzan hadn't left so that he could stop these evil men.

Clayton even caught Kerchak, but not for long. The net was not strong enough to hold him and Kerchak broke free. Clayton saw the gorilla escape.

"I remember you," he said. "I think this one would be better off stuffed."

As soon as Tarzan was freed, he dove into the water and swam for shore. He and his friends got to the gorillas as quickly as they could. They arrived just in time to find Clayton threatening Kerchak. Tarzan rushed to his leader's side.

"You came back," Kerchak said, surprised.

"I came home," answered Tarzan.

While Kerchak, Tantor, Tarzan, and Terk fought off the men, Jane rushed to free Kala. She swung on a vine and knocked over one of the sailors who was carrying Kala's cage. The man holding the other side of the cage came after her, but then a small baboon appeared. It was the same baby baboon Jane had met in the jungle…and he had his friends with him. The man ran for his life from the stampeding baboons.

Jane tried to free Kala, but she couldn't open the cage. Just then, Tarzan appeared with a crowbar in hand. Then just as they pried open the cage, they heard a shot.

It was Clayton, and he had wounded Tarzan in the arm. Kerchak heard the shot and came to Tarzan's defense. He charged at Clayton, roaring as loud as he could. But Clayton wounded Kerchak, who fell to the ground.

Tarzan led Clayton high up into the tree canopy. After a fight, Tarzan managed to grab Clayton's gun.

"Go ahead, shoot me," said Clayton. "Be a man."

"Not a man like you!" cried Tarzan, breaking the gun and throwing it down.

They struggled, and Clayton got tangled up in some vines. He chopped at them to free himself, but he cut one too many and fell to his death.

Tarzan went to his ape father's side. "Kerchak, forgive me," he said.

"No, forgive me for not understanding that you have always been one of us. Our family will look to you now," whispered Kerchak. "Take care of them, my son."

All the gorillas hung their heads as Kerchak took his last breath.

The next day Tarzan went down to the beach to say goodbye to Jane.

"London will seem so small compared to all this," she said.

Tarzan put his hand to hers. Then Jane got into the rowboat, and the captain started to row them away.

"Jane, dear, I can't help feeling that you should stay," Professor Porter said. And when Jane started to object, her father said, "You love him."

As she looked back at Tarzan standing on the beach, Jane knew that her father was right. She jumped out of the boat and waded back to Tarzan.

Then Professor Porter followed his daughter. "Tell them that you never found us," he yelled to the captain as he undid his bow tie, preparing to jump into the water after Jane. "After all, people get lost in the jungle every day."

Jane stepped onto the beach to greet her new gorilla family.

Tantor and Tarzan's gorilla family cheered as they watched Jane and Tarzan embrace.

"Ou-ou-ee-eh-ooo," she said to all the gorillas. She and her father were staying!

They knew that Tarzan would never be happy out of the jungle. And now that he had met her, he would never be happy without Jane, either. Tarzan and Jane swung through the forest on vines, and slid along the mossy branches together.

And so, from then on, Tarzan and Jane lived happily in the jungle.

Disney's THE LION KING II
SIMBA'S·PRIDE

It was a special day at Pride Rock. Animals had gathered from far and wide to greet the Lion King's new cub.

As the winds swirled majestically, Rafiki, the wise mystic baboon, held the infant high so the animals of the Pride Lands could admire their beloved king's new baby. The proud parents, Simba and Nala, nuzzled each other as they watched the ancient ceremony.

Simba's old friends, Timon and Pumbaa, were almost as excited as the new parents. "Look at the little guy," Timon gushed. "A chip off the old block."

Just then, Rafiki made an announcement. "It is a girl!"

Simba and Nala beamed with pride.

"Girl?" yelled Timon, who was not known for his diplomacy. "Oy!"

That evening, Rafiki retired alone to his tree to paint a picture of Simba's new daughter, Kiara. Then he looked to the skies and the spirit of his dear old friend, Mufasa.

"Oh, Mufasa," Rafiki chanted, "another circle of life is complete!"

But in response, Mufasa made a wind blow that rattled the trees. He was warning Rafiki that trouble was brewing nearby.

Long ago, the great king Mufasa had been killed by the treacherous act of his own brother, Scar. Scar had led a renegade group of lions who tried to seize control of the Pride Lands.

His plot had failed, and Mufasa's son, Simba, had taken his rightful place as king.

Now Scar was dead, but his lioness Zira had not lost her thirst for power...at any cost.

Zira and the other Outsiders lived in the Outlands, a dry and barren place where Mufasa had banished them when they began making trouble. Now, Zira was plotting to avenge Scar's death. She was training her son Kovu to take Simba's place as king of the Pride Lands. She was bringing Kovu up to be strong and ruthless.

As a first step, she sent Kovu's brother and sister, Nuka and Vitani, on a mission to find out what was happening at Pride Rock.

"Simba's new cub is a girl!" Vitani reported.

Zira smiled. "Boys," she growled, "will be kings."

"Since I am the oldest…maybe I should be the king!" said Nuka.

"Don't be a fool, Nuka!" Zira snarled. Under Zira's plan, everyone had a role to play. Her favorite child, Kovu, would be king. Nuka and Vitani were to protect him.

Several months later, Kiara had grown into a happy and healthy young cub, always ready to play…and eager to explore the world.

"…And remember," Simba lectured his daughter one day as she prepared to go out and play, "stay in sight of Pride Rock at all times. And stay away from the Outlands."

Kiara promised to be careful and then raced away.

But Simba had a feeling that his daughter was in the mood for adventure. So he asked his friends Timon and Pumbaa to follow her and make sure she was safe.

Kiara was not at all pleased when she realized that she had two baby-sitters following her around.

But Kiara was a clever cub. She waited until Timon and Pumbaa started bickering. Once they were distracted, she slipped away to explore on her own.

After wandering for a while, Kiara noticed a swampy river she had never seen before. Fascinated, she scampered happily down a steep slope towards the water.

There she came face to face with a strange cub from the Outlands.

Kiara was startled to see a stranger. She remembered her father's warnings about the Outsiders, so she turned on her heels to get away and scrambled across some large rocks at the swamp's edge.

Then, to Kiara's dismay, one of the rocks she was standing on moved! It was a crocodile! And there were more all around her, with hungry jaws snapping.

Kiara froze with terror. Then the strange cub reappeared suddenly at her side, and together they scrambled across the backs of the crocodiles to the safety of the water's edge.

"You were really brave!" Kiara said when the cubs were safe.

"You were pretty brave, too," the other cub said hesitantly. "My name's Kovu."

"I'm Kiara."

Neither cub knew that the lioness Zira was spying on them. And she didn't like what she saw. As Zira watched, she realized that Kiara had lost her fear of Kovu—and that the two cubs were becoming friends. Kiara even tried to start a game of tag, but Kovu didn't know how to play.

Just then, Simba appeared. He had been looking everywhere for Kiara, and when he saw her with the cub from the Outlands, he sprang to defend her.

Immediately Zira emerged from her hiding place to stand beside her son. "Simba," she hissed at her old enemy.

Zira was about to attack when she heard a growl from behind her. It was Kiara's mother, Nala. Behind her were Timon and Pumbaa. If Zira tried to fight now, she would be badly outnumbered.

Instead, she coyly introduced Kovu as Scar's chosen heir—and the next leader of the Pride Lands.

Simba understood the threat. He knew that Zira had not accepted Scar's defeat. "Take him and get out," he said. "We're finished here."

"Oh, no," Zira replied slyly. "We have barely begun." Then she and Kovu headed back towards the Outlands.

As Simba picked up Kiara to take her home to Pride Rock, the two cubs quietly bid each other goodbye. They would miss playing together. Their friendship seemed to be over before it had even begun.

When Simba and Kiara were alone, the Lion King said, "You need to be careful. As future queen—"

"What if I don't want to be queen?" Kiara replied. She looked at a bird flying free overhead. She was not sure she wanted all the responsibility of being a ruler of the Pride Lands.

Simba understood her. So he explained patiently, "That's like saying you don't want to be a lion. It's in your blood. As I am. We are part of each other."

Meanwhile, in the Outlands, Zira lashed out at Nuka, who had failed to keep an eye on his brother, Kovu.

"It's not his fault," Kovu interrupted. "I went off on my own." Then he started talking about Kiara. "She didn't seem so bad. I thought we could be friends."

"Friends?" Zira hissed. Then she paused. Maybe Kovu had an idea. The way to overthrow Simba was through his daughter. She would allow Kovu to get close to the future queen. Then Kovu would be able to get rid of Simba and take over the Pride Lands.

One day, after seasons had passed, Kovu stood proudly in front of the Outsiders while his mother inspected him carefully. "You are ready," Zira pronounced. The other Outsiders roared their approval.

Meanwhile, on Pride Rock, Kiara was preparing to make her first solo hunt.

"Daddy," Kiara said, as she started out toward the plains. "You have to promise that you'll let me do this on my own. Promise?"

Simba promised, but soon after Kiara left, he realized that he could not bear the thought of his daughter facing any danger on her own. In recent days, there had been growing tension between the Pride Landers and the Outsiders. He suspected that Zira was up to something.

Simba knew he had to break his promise to Kiara. Once again, he asked Timon and Pumbaa to follow Kiara and make sure she stayed out of trouble.

Timon and Pumbaa took their mission seriously. They did their best to protect Kiara without letting her know they were nearby. They ducked behind rocks, scooted behind trees, and crawled on their bellies through the tall grass. Then they came face to face with…

…Kiara!

Kiara felt betrayed and angry. Her father had promised to let her hunt on her own. But he didn't trust her after all!

She raced away from Timon and Pumbaa as fast as she could. The warthog and the meerkat had no chance of keeping up with the young lioness.

Unfortunately, Kiara was running right into a trap that Zira had prepared for her.

Zira's spies had been keeping a constant watch on events at Pride Rock. They had told her of Kiara's first big hunting trip. Now it was time to put her evil plan in motion.

She sent Nuka and Vitani to set fire to the long grass where Kiara was planning to hunt.

By the time Kiara noticed the flames closing in on her, it was too late to escape. She was overcome by the smoke and surrounded by fire.

Just when it looked as though Kiara might be lost forever, Kovu appeared. He braved his way through the dense smoke and flames, and dragged Kiara, unconscious, to safety in a nearby swamp.

When Kiara regained consciousness, she was furious. "Why'd you bring me here?" she asked the strange lion who had rescued her. "Who do you think you are?"

Then she paused. He seemed familiar. And so did the swamp where they were standing.

"Kovu?" she asked.

Just then, Simba and Nala arrived with Rafiki. They had seen the fire from Pride Rock, and arrived in time to see the brave rescue.

Still, Simba was suspicious of the young lion. But Kovu stood his ground. "I humbly ask to join your pride," he said.

Simba hesitated. Kovu was an Outsider, but he had just saved Kiara's life.

Reluctantly, Simba allowed Kovu to return to Pride Rock with his family.

But he still did not trust Kovu. That night, Simba would not let him inside his cave with the rest of his pride.

From afar, Nuka and Zira watched, perched on a tree limb, waiting to see what would happen. When they saw Kiara come out of the cave to speak to Kovu, they hoped to see him get rid of Kiara and her father once and for all. But after a few minutes, Kiara went quietly back into the cave.

That night, Simba had a horrible dream about the day Scar had let Mufasa fall to his death. But in the dream, he saw Kovu instead of Scar. Simba couldn't help wondering about whether Kovu could be trusted.

Simba had reason to worry. Kovu had spent his whole life in training to destroy the Lion King. But the next day, as Kovu lay in wait to attack Simba, something made him hesitate.

It was Kiara. She wanted him to go with her to the plains, and teach her how to stalk.

They came across Timon and Pumbaa, hunting for bugs as usual, and having a hard time because there were so many birds around. Kiara and Kovu decided to help, racing around, scaring the birds away. One bird even gave Timon an unexpected ride.

For the first time in his life, Kovu was actually having fun!

The friends spent the rest of the day enjoying themselves—chasing birds, and annoying a herd of rhinoceroses.

"You're okay, kid," Timon said to Kovu, which made the young lion feel quite special. Even more important, he realized how much he enjoyed spending time with Kiara.

That night, Kovu and Kiara lay on their backs under the stars, gazing up at the vast expanse of sky.

"My father and I used to do this all the time," Kiara said. "He says all the great kings of the past are up there."

Kovu had spent his whole life believing that the Pride Landers were his enemies. Now, he was beginning to doubt everything Zira had taught him.

On a nearby hill, Simba was also having doubts. "Father," he said, "I am lost. Kovu is Scar's heir. How can I accept him?"

But there were no answers from his father that night.

Instead Nala appeared at Simba's side. She suggested that Simba get to know Kovu better. Maybe Kovu would choose to follow a different path from the one Zira and Scar had chosen.

Rafiki also hoped that Kovu would decide to stay with the Pride Landers. The baboon had been getting messages in the wind from his friend Mufasa, telling him that Kiara and Kovu belonged together.

At first, Rafiki didn't like the idea. But when he saw Kiara and Kovu nuzzling, he knew they were falling in love. And he understood Mufasa's wise message.

That night, when Kiara and Kovu returned to Pride Rock from their day of adventure, Simba finally invited the young lion to join the rest of the pride inside their cave.

From a safe distance, Vitani was spying on her brother and saw him enter the cave. This wasn't part of the Outsiders' plan! She raced to tell Zira.

Zira was outraged when she heard what had happened. "Kovu cannot betray us!" she cried.

This was the moment Nuka had been waiting for. "When the time comes, he'll show his true colors. I have a plan," he said slyly.

Nuka so desperately wanted Zira's approval that he would do anything to outshine Kovu.

The next day, Simba invited Kovu to go for a walk so he could explain the history between the Pride Landers and the Outsiders. Scar, he said, had never been able to let go of the hatred in his heart. In the end, it had destroyed him. But it had also destroyed his own brother, Mufasa.

This was the first time Kovu had heard the truth about his family. He was disappointed to learn about his Uncle Scar, but he realized that Simba was right. The hatred had to stop.

Just then, Simba heard a noise, and turned to see Zira and several other Outsiders advancing in a circle toward him.

It was an ambush! And Simba was certain that Kovu had helped to set it up, especially when Zira congratulated her unsuspecting son.

"Why, Simba," said Zira, "what are you doing out here? And so alone."

Realizing that he was outnumbered Simba raced to escape into a nearby ravine. Then, with nowhere else to go, he scrambled onto a high pile of logs, which were perched precariously on top of each other.

At the top of the pile, Simba was desperately aware that a single wrong step would make the logs fall. And Nuka was the only Outsider foolish enough to advance. "I'll do it. For you, Zira," he said, ready to do anything to gain his mother's affection.

But when Nuka jumped up, the logs began to tumble. Simba quickly leaped to safety. By the time the logs stopped rolling, Nuka lay trapped beneath them.

Zira ran to his side and ran a gentle paw across her son's face as he took his last breath.

Then, in her anger, she turned toward Kovu, and swiped a vicious claw across his face. Forever after that, Kovu would wear a scar above his eye exactly like the one that had marked Scar.

Kovu turned his back on his mother, and returned to Pride Rock. Now he knew where his loyalties lay—with Simba and Kiara.

But when he reached Pride Rock, he met the scorn of thousands of animals. All the Pride Landers thought that Kovu had led Simba into the Outsiders' ambush.

From the top of Pride Rock, Simba pronounced Kovu's fate: exile from the Pride Lands forever. Kiara tried to defend Kovu, but Simba had made up his mind.

Kiara went after Kovu, to convince him to come home. She still believed that together they could bring peace to the Outsiders and the Pride Landers.

But by the time they returned to Pride Rock, a furious battle was already underway. Kiara found her father in the midst of the fray.

"Daddy, this has to stop!" Kiara pleaded. Then she repeated the very words he had once spoken to her. "A wise king once told me," she said, "we are one."

Simba hesitated for only a moment. He remembered what his father had taught him. And then, he called for peace.

Zira was furious at this turn of events. She lunged at Simba, but Kiara jumped to block her attack. Then, snarling and scratching, the two lionesses rolled together to the edge of a cliff. For a moment, it looked as though both would tumble over the edge. But Kiara managed to hold on.

Zira clung to the edge for a few long moments, refusing Kiara's help. Then…

…Zira was lost forever.

The Outsiders laid aside their dream of taking over Simba's territory. Instead, they returned to their old home in the rich Pride Lands, to live in peace and harmony with the Pride Landers.

A few days later, there was much rejoicing at Pride Rock for yet another reason. This time, the Pride Landers and the Outsiders gathered together in a great circle, and watched Rafiki perform the ancient ceremony to mark the union of their two prides.

And so the promise that Mufasa had whispered in the wind had come true. Thanks to Kiara and Kovu, the warring prides had joined together to build a lasting peace.

Together, Simba and Kovu stood with their mates at the edge of Pride Rock and roared their happiness over the plains.

Then Simba heard his father's voice in the wind. "Well done, my son," said Mufasa. The Lion King had brought peace to the Pride Lands once again.

Disney's MULAN

Long ago in China, the Emperor built a Great Wall to protect his country. Soldiers patrolled the wall day and night.

Among the Emperor's many enemies was Shan-Yu, the leader of the Huns. Shan-Yu saw the wall as a challenge. One night, he and his men scaled the wall with ropes, attacking the soldier on duty who barely managed to light the warning torch.

"Now all of China knows you're here," the soldier said to Shan-Yu.

"Perfect," the Hun replied.

When he heard of the attack, the Emperor ordered his counsel, Chi Fu, and General Li to enlist more troops to defend his people.

"A single grain of rice can tip the scale," he said to General Li. "One man may be the difference between victory and defeat."

Meanwhile, in a small village far from the Imperial City, a young girl named Mulan was getting ready to meet the Matchmaker.

As usual, Mulan was running late. She rushed to get all her chores done in time, making a mess of things.

"Mulan," her father, Fa Zhou, said, "we are counting on you to—"

"To uphold the family honor," Mulan interrupted. "Don't worry father, I won't let you down."

Mulan was very nervous as she got ready with the help of her mother and grandmother. She had written notes to herself on the inside of her wrist, and they almost washed off in the bathtub. Just before she left, her mother gave her a comb that was a family heirloom, and her grandmother gave her a cricket named Cri-Kee for good luck.

Mulan was the first girl to be called into the Matchmaker's room. She cheated a bit, reading from the notes on her arm to answer questions. Things were going well until the ink from the notes came off on the Matchmaker. Mulan was so nervous that when she poured the tea, it spilled everywhere. Then she saw that Cri-Kee had gotten out of his cage and was lounging in the cup of tea that the Matchmaker was about to drink.

Mulan tried to take the tea back, but Cri-Kee got into the Matchmaker's dress. The Matchmaker panicked and started to run, but she backed right into the stove and suddenly her dress was on fire. Mulan threw the pot of tea she was holding at the Matchmaker to extinguish the flames.

"You are a disgrace!" the Matchmaker screamed, tea streaming down her face. "You may look like a bride, but you will never bring your family honor!"

Back home, Mulan looked at her reflection in a pool of water and didn't recognize herself. She saw a young woman with perfect hair and make-up, an elegant beauty. She didn't think she could ever be that young woman in the reflection.

Mulan had done the unthinkable—she had brought dishonor on her family. She washed the make-up off her face and let down her hair. She stared down at the comb her mother had given her, as her eyes filled with tears of shame.

Then her father found her and asked her to sit with him under their lotus tree.

"My, my, what beautiful blossoms we have this year," he said, pointing at a branch. "Look, this one's late. But I'll bet that when it blooms, it will be the most beautiful of all."

Mulan knew that he was talking about her, but she couldn't believe him.

Just then, Chi Fu came to announce the Hun invasion. He asked for one man from each household to fight for the Emperor. Mulan's father had no sons so, although he was already injured from a previous war, he stepped forward.

"I am ready to serve the Emperor," Fa Zhou said.

"Please, sir!" Mulan cried out to Chi Fu. "My father has already fought bravely for the Emperor."

Chi Fu was appalled that a young woman could be outspoken.

"Mulan, you dishonor me," her father said. Mulan was not being a proper young lady by speaking up, and as the only man in the family the honorable thing for her father to do was to serve the Emperor.

That night, Mulan saw her father practice using his sword. As he raised it above his head, the pain in his injured leg made him lose his balance and fall. Mulan was very worried—if her father went to war, he would surely die. She went to the family shrine to pray to the Fa Family Ancestors, and then she had an idea.

Returning to the house, Mulan took her father's sword and used it to cut her hair. Then she tied her hair up like a man's and put on her father's armor. In the place of his conscription notice, she left the comb her mother had given her. Then she mounted her horse, Khan, and set off to take her father's place in the army.

In the middle of the night, as thunder roared overhead, Grandmother Fa awoke and realized that Mulan was gone. It was too late to stop her. The entire family was petrified—they knew that the penalty for impersonating a man was death.

"You must go after her!" Mulan's mother said to her father. "She could be killed!"

"If I reveal her," Fa Zhou replied, "she will be."

Mulan's parents held each other and shook with fear as they wondered what to do. For now, it seemed, there was nothing they could do but pray.

Grandmother Fa went to the shrine and called upon the family's ancestors to help them through this crisis.

"Ancestors, hear our prayer," she said. "Watch over Mulan."

The First Ancestor woke up Mushu the dragon. Mushu used to be one of the Fu Family Guardians, but ever since an incident a couple of generations ago, he had been demoted. He kept hoping for a second chance. He tried to volunteer for duty, but the First Ancestor would have none of it.

"*Those* are the Guardians," the First Ancestor said to Mushu, pointing up at the statues at the top of the shrine "*They...*"

"...protect the family." Mushu said humbly. "I ring the gong."

The little dragon banged the gong to awaken the other Ancestors, who argued over what they should do, each one blaming the other for the way that Mulan had turned out.

Finally, they decided that Mushu must awaken the Great Stone Dragon, who stood outside the shrine.

Mushu banged his gong, but the Great Stone Dragon did not budge. So Mushu screamed into the Great Stone Dragon's ear. Suddenly, the Dragon crumbled, until all that was left was a stone head on a large pile of dust.

"Great Stone Dragon, are you awakened?" asked the First Ancestor.

Mushu picked up the stone dragon's head, and held it above his own so that it peeked over the bushes.

"Yes! I just woke up. I am—I am the Great Stone Dragon. Good Morning!" Mushu said in a deep voice. "I'll go forth and fetch Mulan. Did I mention that I was the Great Stone Dragon?"

"Go!" the First Ancestor said. "The fate of the Fa family rests in your claws."

Mushu was sure that he would never be a Guardian again, but Cri-Kee said that he should go get Mulan.

"Go get her? What's the matter with you? After this great stone Humpty Dumpty mess, I'd have to bring her home with a medal to get back in the temple...."

Then Mushu had an idea: If he brought Mulan home as a war hero, the Ancestors would respect him again.

Mushu found Mulan and announced himself. "I have been sent by your ancestors," he said.

Mulan looked down at him, "My ancestors sent a lizard to help me?"

"Dragon," Mushu corrected her.

"You're, uh...tiny," Mulan said skeptically.

"I'm travel-size for your convenience," Mushu replied. Pointing to her horse, Khan, he said, "If I were my real size your cow here would die of fright."

Mulan was still skeptical, but when Mushu threatened to send dishonor on her family, she agreed to take him with her.

At the army camp, Mushu told Mulan how to act like a man. "Time to show them your man walk!" he said. "Shoulders back, chest high, feet apart, head up, and strut!"

Mulan looked around at the other men in the camp and wondered what she had gotten herself into.

"They're disgusting," Mulan said.

"Punch him," Mushu advised, pointing to a soldier. "It's how men say 'hello.'"

When she did, the man punched her back, and before she knew it, Mulan had started a brawl. When the officers emerged from General Li's tent moments later, they found the entire camp in disarray. The other soldiers all fingered Mulan.

"What is your name?" demanded Captain Li Shang.

It took a while for Mulan to think up a boy's name. "Ping!" she said, finally. "My name is Ping."

Shang ordered the whole troop to clean up the mess that night. "Tomorrow, the real work begins," he added.

The soldiers glared at Ping as they did the work.

The next day, Shang shot an arrow to the top of a pole and told the soldiers to retrieve it.

"This represents discipline, and this represents strength," he said, giving them two weights. "You need both to reach the arrow."

Nobody was able to climb the pole. But Mulan worked very hard until one day she managed to reach the arrow by looping the weights together, gaining the respect of the other soldiers.

A few weeks later, Mushu and Cri-Kee forged a letter saying that soldiers were needed at the front, so that Mulan could see battle and become a hero. Shang and his men marched until they came upon a battleground. Imperial soldiers lay dead, including Shang's father, General Li.

"We're the only hope for the Emperor now," Shang said, as he made a shrine out of his father's sword and helmet. "Move out!" he ordered.

The soldiers marched into the snowy mountains when suddenly a rocket went off from within the wagon Khan was leading. From over the next hill arrows came flying. Shang's troops!

"You just gave away our position!" Shang yelled at Mulan. Then he ordered his troops to get out of the Huns' shooting range.

The Imperial soldiers fought back, shooting their rockets at the advancing Huns, who far outnumbered them. It was beginning to look hopeless for Shang's troops.

An idea came to Mulan as she grabbed the last rocket.

Instead of aiming the rocket at Shan-Yu, she pointed it up at the mountain face and lit it with Mushu's fiery breath. The rocket created an avalanche, just as Mulan had hoped. When Shan-Yu saw what Mulan had done, he charged at her with his sword, injuring her. But then he was buried under the snow along with the rest of the Huns. Mulan hurried to escape the oncoming waves of snow.

Mulan saw that Shang was about to be overcome by the avalanche. She rode Khan through the rolling waves of snow, saving him just as they were about to tumble over a cliff. Yao tossed them a rope, and Mulan shot the arrow at the end of the rope to the other soldiers, who pulled her and Shang to safety.

"From now on," Shang said to Ping, "you have my trust."

Mulan put a hand to her chest, and when she pulled it back, she saw blood. Then she blacked out.

When Mulan awoke, Shang was standing near her, with a disapproving look in his eye. Then Chi Fu came in.

"I knew there was something wrong with you!" Chi Fu yelled, tossing her out into the snow. "A woman!"

"I did it to save my father," Mulan said.

"High treason!" Chi Fu continued.

"I didn't mean for it to go this far," Mulan said weakly. "It was the only way."

Chi Fu reminded Shang that the penalty for impersonating a man was death. Taking Mulan's sword, Shang raised it high above his head.

But instead of killing Mulan, Shang just threw the sword down and said, "A life for a life. My debt is repaid."

Then the soldiers marched off, leaving Mulan alone in the snow. Cri-Kee lit a fire with twigs, but it was too small to be of much use. Mulan shivered with cold and wished she had never left home.

"Maybe I didn't go for my father," she mused. "Maybe what I really wanted was to prove that I could do things right, so that when I looked in the mirror, I'd see someone worthwhile.

"But I was wrong. I see nothing," Mulan said, as she picked up her helmet and looked at her reflection in it. "I'm sorry I wasted your time, Mushu."

Mushu answered, "Look, the truth is, we're both frauds. Your ancestors never sent me."

Eventually, Mulan decided it was time to get going. "I'll have to face my father sooner or later," she said. "Let's go home."

Mushu did his best to encourage Mulan. "We started this thing together and that's how we'll finish it," he said.

Mulan picked herself up and started to head home. Then she saw Shan-Yu and some of his men emerging from the snow. They were alive! She knew they were heading towards the Imperial City. She jumped onto Khan and headed in the direction they took.

"Home is that way!" Mushu said, pointing behind them.

"I have to do something!" said Mulan.

When Mulan reminded Mushu of his promise to stick together, he agreed to go with her. "Hee-haw!" he shouted as they headed to save the Emperor.

In the Imperial City, a huge parade was being held for Shang and his soldiers in honor of their victory. Mulan rode up next to her former captain and warned him about the Huns. But Shang wouldn't pay her any attention.

"You don't belong here, Mulan. Go home,"Shang replied coolly.

Mulan tried to tell the other people about the danger, but everyone ignored her because she was just a girl.

Shang presented Shan-Yu's sword to the Emperor, and the crowd cheered. But just then, a falcon swooped down and snatched the sword from the Emperor's grasp. It was Shan-Yu's falcon, and it returned to where Shan-Yu was hiding atop the palace, disguised as one of the gargoyles. Then the dragon that had been dancing for the crowd was thrown aside, and out popped more Huns. They grabbed the Emperor, and ran into the palace, locking the doors behind them.

All seemed lost, but once again Mulan had a plan. Even Shang realized that it was a good idea. She dressed some of her fellow soldiers as women. Shang, Mulan, and the disguised soldiers used Mulan's pole-climbing technique to climb up the columns and into the palace.

Shan-Yu had posted his guards outside the room where he held the Emperor. The guards heard a noise. They opened the door to Mulan and her friends.

Look how ugly these women are, thought the guards.

The women winked and fluttered their eyelashes awkwardly at the guards, holding up their fans as daintily as they could. The Huns let down their guard and allowed the women to approach.

Then, when they were close enough, the well-trained Imperial soldiers attacked the Huns.

"Shang, go!" Mulan cried.

Shang slipped past the Huns and raced up the stairs and into the room where the Emperor was being held by Shan-Yu.

Meanwhile, Shan-Yu ordered the Emperor to bow to him, but the old man wouldn't budge. "No matter how the wind howls, the mountain cannot bow to it," he said to the Hun.

"Then you will kneel in pieces," said Shan-Yu with his sword raised.

Just then, Shang burst in to the room with his sword drawn, challenging Shan-Yu. They struggled and Shang managed to pin Shan-Yu down. Then Mulan and the other soldiers entered.

With Shan-Yu out of the way, Chien-Po grabbed the Emperor and used his sash to slide down a rope to the ground.

Shan-Yu was enraged to see the Emperor escape. He wanted to take his revenge on Shang, but when Mulan revealed that she was the soldier from the mountain, who had defeated his army, he ran after her instead.

Mulan led Shan-Yu up onto the palace roof while Mushu led Cri-Kee to the nearby fireworks tower.

With only a fan for a weapon, Mulan managed to avoid Shan-Yu's sword, and grab it from him.

Then Mulan used the sword to pin the Hun to the roof, just as Mushu rode a rocket at him. Mushu jumped off the rocket just in time, but Shan-Yu had nowhere to go. He was launched into the tower where all the fireworks were stored. Color and light lit up the sky.

The Emperor thanked Mulan in front of the cheering crowd. "You have saved us all," he said, and then bowed. Mulan bowed back, and he offered her a position on his council.

"With all due respect, your excellency," Mulan replied, "I think I've been away from home long enough."

The Emperor gave her a medallion with his crest on it, "So your family will know what you have done for me." Then he handed her Shan-Yu's sword, "So that the world will know what you have done for China."

Shang stood beside the Emperor as they watched Mulan leave.

"The flower that blooms in adversity is the most rare and beautiful of all," the Emperor said.

When Shang didn't understand what he meant, he added, "You don't meet a girl like that every dynasty!"

Mulan brought her father the medallion and the sword. "They're gifts," she said, "to honor the Fa family."

"The greatest gift and honor," her father replied, "is having you for a daughter."

Just then, Shang appeared at the gate. He said he was bringing back Mulan's helmet.

"Would you like to stay for dinner?" Mulan offered.

"Dinner would be fine," Shang said.

Meanwhile, in the shrine, Mushu was saying to the proud ancestors, "Come on—who did a good job?"

"Oh, all right, you can be a Guardian again," said the First Ancestor.

"All right!" exclaimed Mushu, and all the Ancestors celebrated.

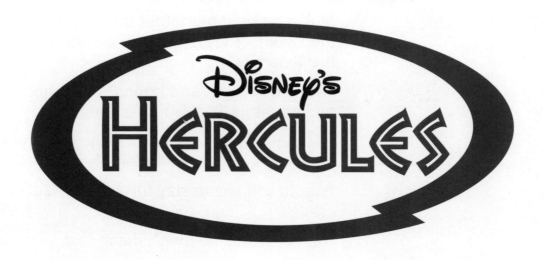

This is the story of Hercules, a great hero and the strongest man who ever walked the earth. But our story begins long before his birth....

Long ago, in ancient Greece, powerful gods ruled the Earth from their sanctuary on Mount Olympus.

The greatest of the gods by far was the mighty Zeus. Zeus organized the rest of the gods to conquer the evil Titans, gigantic troublemakers who had caused great chaos—tormenting the people with catastrophic earthquakes, tidal waves, and volcanic blasts.

But now, the Titans were safely locked away where they could do no more harm. Under the wise guidance of Zeus, the earth was a peaceful and orderly place, and the people were happy. So were the gods.

So of course there was great celebration when a son was born to Zeus and his beautiful wife, the goddess Hera. The baby Hercules was bathed in a heavenly glow, and wore a gold medallion.

When news of Hercules' birth spread, all of the gods and goddesses gathered at Zeus's palace to admire the new baby, and to shower him with a mountain of fabulous gifts.

Zeus was very proud of his son.

Especially when the baby grabbed hold of his father's finger, and lifted him right off the ground!

"This child is strong, just like his dad!" laughed Zeus.

Then Hera nudged her husband, "Where's *our* gift, dear?"

Zeus formed a puff of clouds with his hands and spun the clouds into the shape of a baby horse. Out stepped a colt with white wings.

"His name is Pegasus, Son," said Zeus. "And he's all yours." Baby Hercules cooed and gurgled and stretched out his arms.

Meanwhile, Hades, god of the Underworld, had arrived at the party and was watching with a fierce scowl. Hades was not exactly crazy about Zeus and his happy little family. Thanks to Zeus, Hades was in charge of the gloomy Underworld. While the other gods whooped it up on Mount Olympus, he had to spend his time surrounded by a bunch of lost souls and dead-heads. On top of that, he had to put up with a giant three-headed guard dog that kept attacking him, as well as some very annoying demons

So by the time Hades got home to the Underworld, he had figured out what he wanted...revenge!

Two demons, Pain and Panic, were waiting for him on the dock. "Let me know the instant the Fates arrive," Hades growled.

The Fates were three ugly crones who shared only one eye between them but could see the future. "So let me just ask...is this Hercules—is this kid gonna mess up my hostile takeover bid or what?" Hades demanded.

The Fates were not supposed to reveal the future to anyone, but Hades wormed the truth out of them.

They told him that in 18 years, when the planets lined up, he would have his only chance to take over the world. But, they warned, "should Hercules fight, you will fail."

"WHAT?" Hades exploded. When he calmed down, he remembered the rules. No one could kill a god—gods are immortal. He would have to make Hercules mortal.

So he gave the demons Pain and Panic a magic potion and sent them off to kidnap the baby Hercules.

Hercules found the ride through the night air quite a lot of fun. But when the demons landed on Earth, Hercules yelled.

Hercules' cry wakened a farmer and his wife, and they dashed outdoors to see what was going on. "Who's there?" the farmer called into the darkness.

Pain and Panic dropped Hercules before he had finished the potion and hid themselves behind some bushes.

"Why you poor thing," the wife said when she saw the baby. Because of the potion, Hercules had already lost his god-like glow. He looked like a normal baby—and the couple had been praying for a child for a long time.

"Amphitryon, for so many years we prayed to the gods to bless us with a child. Perhaps they've answered our prayers," the farmer said. Then he noticed the gold medallion the baby wore. "Hercules," he read.

Pain and Panic knew they had to finish their job. But when they changed into snakes and slithered out from the bushes to attack the farmer and his wife, baby Hercules snatched them up by their snaky tails, tied them together in a knot, and hurled them screaming far into the distance. The farmer and his wife stared at him in amazement.

Panic said. "Hades is gonna kill us when he finds out what happened!"

"You mean *if* he finds out," said Pain.

Meanwhile, Hercules had become almost mortal. But because he had not finished the potion, he kept his god-like strength.

He grew up thinking that Amphitryon and his wife were his parents. But his enormous strength sometimes created problems. When he tried to join a group of boys playing a game of discus in the village, he accidentally bumped into some stone pillars, and destroyed the marketplace.

"**D**estructo-boy," the townspeople called him. "What a geek!" they shouted. "Freak!" They wanted Hercules' father to keep him away from them. "That boy is a menace!" someone said.

Back home, the farmer said, "Son, you shouldn't let those things they said back there get to you."

"But, Pop, they're right. I am a freak!" Hercules hung his head. "Sometimes I feel like…like I really don't belong here. Like I'm supposed to be someplace else."

The farmer and his wife knew it was time to tell Hercules the truth. They told him how they had found him as a baby, and they showed him the gold medallion. "This was around your neck when we found you. It's the symbol of the gods."

Hercules realized that he had to find out where he came from—to find a place where he fit in. "Maybe the gods have the answers," he said. He put the medallion around his neck, and said goodbye to the only parents he knew. "You're the greatest parents anyone could have, but I gotta know…."

So Hercules traveled to the temple of Zeus. He prayed before a huge statue. "Oh, mighty Zeus, please hear me and answer my prayer. I need to know. Who am I? Where do I belong?"

With a flash of lightning the statue came alive. Hercules was terrified, and tried to run away, but Zeus picked the boy up.

"Is this the kind of 'hello' you give your father?" Zeus said.

Hercules was astonished. "F-f-father?" he stammered. "If you're my father, that would make me a…"

"A god," Zeus said. And he told Hercules the whole story, about how he was kidnapped and became mortal. The problem was, he explained, that Hercules could not return to Mount Olympus because he was no longer immortal.

"You can't do a thing?" Hercules asked.

"I can't, Hercules. But you can," Zeus replied. "If you can prove yourself a *true hero* on Earth, your godhood will be restored."

"Great!" Hercules said. "Uh…exactly how do you become a true hero?"

The first step, Zeus explained, was to find Philoctetes, the trainer of heroes.

Hercules was so eager to begin that he ran for the door. "Whoa! Hold your horses!" Zeus said. "Which reminds me…"

Zeus whistled, and a great white winged horse flew in from the sky. "You probably don't remember Pegasus," Zeus said.

But as soon as the horse nuzzled Hercules, he found he did remember. He mounted Pegasus, and together they flew into the sky.

Philocetes was a tubby little fellow with the horns and hind legs of a goat. "Call me Phil," the satyr said.

"I need your help," Hercules said. "I want to become a hero. A *true* hero."

"Sorry, kid. I can't help ya," Phil said. "Two words: I am retired."

Phil was tired of training heroes; they all ended up disappointing him. But he changed his mind when Zeus hit him with a lightning bolt. So the next day, Hercules began learning all of the skills a hero needs. And he and Phil became good friends.

After months of training, it was time for Hercules to test his skills in real life. "We're going to Thebes," Phil said. "It's a big, tough town. Good place to start building a rep."

But on the way, Hercules and Pegasus heard the cry of a damsel in distress. Hercules rushed to help her. The young woman was struggling to free herself from the clutches of a huge, shaggy centaur—half man and half horse.

Strangely, the woman didn't seem to want help. "Back off!" she said. "I can handle this." But after a struggle, Hercules walloped the centaur.

"Are you all right, Miss, uh…?" Hercules asked shyly.

"Megara. My friends call me Meg," she said, batting her eyelashes.

Megara refused Hercules' offer of a ride, and he watched her walk away. "She's something. Isn't she, Phil?" he said.

"Yeah," answered Phil. "A real pain in the patella!" Then Phil reminded Hercules that they were supposed to be in Thebes.

As Hercules, Phil, and Pegasus continued on their way to Thebes, Megara headed deep into the woods until Hades appeared. "What exactly happened here?" he asked. "I thought you were going to persuade the River Guardian to join my team for the uprising...."

"Look, it wasn't my fault," Meg pleaded. "It was this Wonder Boy, Hercules."

"Hercules?!" Hades shouted, grabbing Pain and Panic by their tails. "So you took care of him, eh?

"Fortunately for the three of you," Hades growled, "we still have time to correct this." Hades had already come up with another plan to get rid of Hercules.

When Hercules and Phil finally got to Thebes, the streets were filled with people, all complaining about the state of their city. Crime was on the rise, and there were floods, fires, and earthquakes.

Of course, Hercules offered to help. "I'm Hercules, and, uh…I happen to be a hero," he said.

But no one took him seriously. In fact, they laughed, which angered Phil. He tried to convince them that Hercules was the real thing, but the crowd laughed ever harder. Finally, Phil butted one man with his horns. Hercules had to break up the fight.

Just then, Hercules heard a voice calling, "Help, please! There's been a terrible accident!"

It was Meg. She explained that two little boys had been trapped by a rock slide.

They climbed onto Pegasus and flew to where the boys were pinned beneath a gigantic boulder. Hercules lifted it easily, and the children scampered away.

Little did Hercules know that Meg had led him into a trap. The boys were really Pain and Panic in disguise. The next moment, Hercules was attacked by a dragon-like monster. The Hydra had been lying in wait behind the boulder.

The Hydra swallowed Hercules in one gulp, but he slashed his way out with his sword, and then sliced off the creature's giant head.

By this time a crowd had gathered, and they cheered wildly. But then Hercules heard a hissing sound from the monster's neck. Out popped three heads where one had been!

Every time Hercules sliced off a head, three more grew to replace it. Finally the monster had thirty heads—all chomping and hissing!

This wasn't working. Hercules stopped to think. Then he smashed his fist into the mountainside and caused a landslide that buried the Hydra and Hercules both.

Phil was devastated. The crowd was silent…and then Hercules emerged from the rubble, and the crowd went wild.

From that day on, people cheered when Hercules rode past. The merchants of Thebes sold souvenirs depicting his victory. Hercules continued his heroics, battling monsters and overcoming disasters wherever he found them, his faithful friend Phil at his side.

After a string of successes, Hercules felt certain he had proven himself. So he and Pegasus traveled to Mount Olympus to see his father.

Zeus looked pleased with what Hercules reported. "You're doing great, son," he said.

"I've been waiting for this day a long time," Hercules said.

"Hmmm, what day is that, son?" asked Zeus.

"The day I rejoin the gods."

A shadow crossed Zeus's face, "My boy, I'm afraid being famous isn't the same as being a true hero."

"What more can I do?"

"Look inside your heart," said Zeus.

Hercules was frustrated. He lost interest in the job of being a hero. So when Meg showed up and suggested that he play hooky from the hero business for a day, Hercules was happy to agree. He never suspected that Hades was behind her visit.

Hades was running out of time. The day the Fates had predicted was approaching—the day the planets would be in perfect alignment and Hades could take over the world.

Only Hercules stood in his way. And Hades still had not discovered the hero's fatal weakness. In fact, so far, Hercules had evaded every trap Hades had set for him.

Meg had had enough of helping Hades. "I've done my part," she said.

That's when Hades reminded her that she had sold him her soul. He offered Meg her freedom in return for her cooperation.

So Meg had set out to discover Hercules' fatal weakness. But her heart wasn't in it.

Hercules and Meg spent a glorious day together, wandering through his gardens and chatting. By evening, Hercules knew he was falling in love with her, and confessed his deepest hopes and fears.

"When I'm with you, I don't feel so…alone," he admitted.

Meg's problem was that she was also falling in love with Hercules. She didn't want to hurt him, but Hades had her in his power. What could she do?

"**G**et yourself another girl," Meg told Hades.

But Hades wouldn't allow Meg to stop working for him. And Phil happened to hear enough of the conversation to figure out that Meg had been working for Hades. He raced to warn Hercules.

"She's a fraud!" Phil cried "She's nothing but a two-timing, no-good, lying—"

"Shut up!" Hercules shouted.

Phil stormed off. "That's it."

So Hercules was alone when Hades showed up with Meg, tightly bound in chains of cloud. "Give up your strength for about twenty-four hours," Hades said, "and Meg here is free as a bird and safe from harm."

Hercules couldn't bear to see Meg suffer. He agreed to the deal, and the next thing he knew, Hades had drained the power from his body.

As he released Meg, Hades told Hercules that she had been working for him all along.

Hades had only twenty-four hours left, and lots to do. First, he released the Titans from the pit where Zeus had imprisoned them. "Look at your squalid prison. Who put you down there?"

"Zeus!" the Titans roared.

"And if I release you, what's the first thing you're gonna do?"

"Destroy him!"

Next, Hades went to find the giant one-eyed Cyclops. "I have a *special* job for you," he said.

So the Titans attacked Mount Olympus. The gods barely had time to prepare themselves for battle. Zeus knew Hades was behind the attack, but he was powerless against the Titans.

The Cyclops was on the rampage in Thebes and the terrified citizens called for help as they tried to get away from the monster.

Hercules headed for the commotion. "Stop!" Meg shouted. "Without your strength, you'll be killed!" But Hercules, convinced that Meg had betrayed him, didn't care whether he lived or died.

Meg went to find Phil. Maybe *he* could talk some sense into Hercules.

By the time Meg returned with Phil, Hercules was battered and dazed, and had nearly given up. But Phil urged him on. "Come on, kid! Fight back," he shouted. "Giving up is for rookies."

So with his last shred of strength, Hercules wrapped a rope around the giant's ankles and toppled him into the sea.

As the Cyclops fell, he knocked over two huge columns. "Hercules! Look out!" Meg cried, pushing Hercules out of the way. One column fell on Meg, pinning her underneath it.

As Hercules strained to move it, he felt his strength returning. It was because Hades had broken his deal—he had promised Meg would be safe, but now she was badly injured. Hercules held her in his arms. "Meg, why did you…? You didn't have to—"

"People always do crazy things when they're in love," Meg whispered. Hercules was speechless. "You can still stop Hades," Meg added.

So Hercules and Pegasus sped to Mount Olympus, leaving Phil to look after Meg. They arrived to find the gods already in chains, tormented by the Titans.

Hercules broke the gods' bonds, saying, "This ought to even up the odds."

Then he smashed through the frozen lava that imprisoned Zeus. "Thank you, my boy," Zeus said. "Now watch your old man work." Grabbing a load of thunderbolts, he hurled them at the Titans.

The Titans shrieked and tried to scatter, but Hercules hurled them into space.

An angry Hades watched from his chariot. "At least I got one swell consolation prize," he called to Hercules. "A friend of yours who's *dying* to see me."

Meg! Hercules jumped onto Pegasus, praying he wouldn't be too late.

But when he landed backed in Thebes, Phil's tearful face told the whole story. Meg was dead. "I'm sorry kid, but there's some things ya just can't change."

"Yes, I can," Hercules vowed.

Back in the Underworld, Hades was still fuming about his defeat when the gates of the throne room burst open, and in came Hercules, riding on the three-headed watchdog, Cerberus.

"Where's Meg?" Hercules demanded. Through an archway, he caught sight of a swirling mass of souls, Meg among them. He reached out his hand, but pulled back in horror. His hand had begun to age.

"You like making deals," Hercules said. "Take me in Meg's place."

Hades considered. "Okay. You get her out, she goes, you stay."

Hercules dived into the Pit of Death. As he swam after Meg, his body aged until he was hardly more than a skeleton. Then, to Hades' amazement, Hercules' body turned back to normal, and began to glow. He emerged from the pit carrying Meg's soul.

"You can't be alive!" Hades said, "You'd have to be…"

"A god?" chimed Pain and Panic.

Hades tried to make another deal, but Hercules just grabbed him and threw him into the Pit of Death.

Hercules guided Meg's spirit back to her lifeless body. As Phil and Pegasus looked on, her eyelids fluttered, then opened. Hercules helped her to her feet.

As they held each other, lightning bolts struck the ground around them, and a cloud billowed beneath their feet. The cloud rose slowly upward, and carried them to the gates of Mount Olympus.

As Hercules started up the stairs, all the gods gave him a standing ovation.

The goddess Hera greeted him. "Hercules, we're so proud of you."

The goddess hugged him. "You were willing to give your life to rescue this young woman…" she said.

"…for a true hero isn't measured by the size of his strength but by the strength of his heart," Zeus said. "Now, at last, my son, you can come home."

Meg looked up at Hercules, tears in her eyes. "Congratulations, Wonder Boy. You'll make one heck of a god."

Hercules had always dreamed of this moment, but it took him only a heartbeat to make his decision.

He turned to his father. "A life without Meg, even an immortal one, would be…empty," he said. He took Meg's hands, and she brightened through her tears. "I wish to stay on Earth with her. I finally know where I belong."

Zeus and Hera were disappointed at losing their son, but they respected his wishes.

In the heavens, Zeus formed a new constellation of stars in the sky, to honor his heroic son.

And Hercules at last knew what his father had meant: heroic deeds are born in the heart.

DISNEY PIXAR

a bug's
life

On Ant Island, the ants were busy preparing their annual offering to the grasshoppers. They all pitched in, collecting grain and bringing it to the offering stone.

Flik worked too, but he didn't do things the way the other ants did. He invented a harvester to pick the grain faster. Even though it worked pretty well, the harvester unfortunately threw an empty stalk right on Atta, the princess of the colony. Flik apologized—he was horrified that he could have hurt the princess. He had wanted so much to impress her, not hurt her. But Atta was not at all impressed with the goofy inventor ant who never seemed to work.

Flik walked away feeling defeated, but Princess Atta's younger sister, Dot, followed him. She told him that she liked his invention.

"Well, you're the first," Flik replied. "I'm beginning to think nothing I do works."

"Me neither," said Dot, who also felt like a failure. Her mother had just told her she was too little to fly. She felt as if her wings would never grow in.

Flik explained to Dot that just as a tiny seed can grow into a giant tree, she would do great things someday. "You just have to give yourself some time," he said.

Suddenly, the alarm sounded and all the ants panicked. The grasshoppers were coming!

The Queen said, "Okay, everyone, single file! Food to the offering stone and into the anthill."

Everybody else hurried into the anthill, but Flik lagged behind because his harvester was too heavy and clumsy. But when he passed by the offering stone, the harvester knocked the entire offering off a cliff!

When the grasshoppers saw the empty offering stone, they got very angry and stormed into the anthill.

"Where's my food?" Hopper, their leader, demanded.

When Princess Atta couldn't answer, Hopper grabbed Dot to show he meant business. But Flik stood up and said, "Leave her alone!"

"It seems to me that you ants are forgetting your place," said Hopper. Then he told them the grasshoppers would be back when the last leaf fell, and he wanted *double* the usual amount of food.

When the grasshoppers left, the Council met to figure out what to do with Flik. He had ruined everything!

Then Flik had one of his ideas. "We could find bigger bugs to come here and fight and forever rid us of Hopper and his gang," he said.

The other ants thought he was crazy, but they let him leave the colony in search of bigger bugs. It would keep him out of trouble and besides, they didn't think he'd ever come back.

Only Dot believed in him. "You just watch," she said to her friends as Flik flew away on a dandelion puff. "He's going to get the bestest, roughest bugs you ever seen!"

Meanwhile, in The City, things weren't going well for P.T. Flea and his circus bugs. They had a rough audience, which heckled and made fun of the performers. Then a couple of flies made fun of Francis the male ladybug, who threatened to beat them up.

Desperate, P.T. decided to call for the grand finale.

The bugs all got ready. This act was supposed to salvage their show, but everything went wrong, and P.T. Flea ended up getting burnt to a crisp.

The audience roared with delight, but P.T. Flea was not pleased at all.

"You're all fired!" he screamed at the circus bugs.

Meanwhile, as the circus bugs were drowning their sorrows in a nearby bug bar, Flik finally arrived in The City. He saw so many bugs that he was sure he'd find someone to help his colony. He went into the bug bar—it looked like the kind of place where tough bugs would hang out.

Soon the circus bugs got involved in a huge brawl inside the tin can bar. When the fighting calmed down, they heard someone clapping. It was Flik.

"I have been scouting for bugs with your exact talents!" Flik cried. "Please, will you help us?"

Flik thought the circus bugs were warriors. The circus bugs thought that Flik was a talent scout, and that he wanted them to entertain the grasshoppers. They were happy to get away from the bugs that were after them.

"We'll take the job," said Slim the walking stick. "You can explain the details on the way."

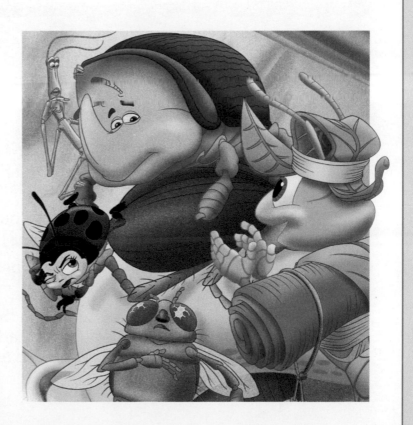

As they approached Ant Island, Flik and the circus bugs could see the hungry, tired ants working harder than ever before.

Dot was the first one to spot Flik coming. "Flik…I knew you could do it!" she cried.

"He wasn't supposed to actually find someone!" said a surprised Princess Atta.

The other ants were scared of the new arrivals.

"We're losing the job," Slim said to his circus buddies when he saw the ants' reaction.

Then Francis spoke up. "When your grasshopper friends get here," he said, "we are gonna knock 'em dead!"

The bugs finally won the ants over. But when the ants gave a party to welcome the "warriors", the circus bugs realized that there had been a misunderstanding. They pulled Flik aside, and told him that they'd have to leave.

Flik begged the circus bugs to stay and help him. He told them that if he failed at this, he would be labeled a loser for the rest of his life, and the whole colony would be in danger. The bugs were trying to sneak off, when suddenly Flik turned to run. "A bird!" he cried.

To make matters worse, Dot had followed Flik. She was flying through the air, holding onto a dandelion puff just as the bird appeared. All the other bugs ran to hide, just as some ants spotted Dot from the safety of a far away ledge.

The Queen and Princess Atta gasped as the bird went after Dot. She let go of the puff just in time to avoid getting swallowed by the bird, but then fell through the air.

Luckily, Francis saw Dot falling, and flew up to rescue her. They landed in a crack in the river bed, with the bird still after them. When the bird landed, it showered them with stones. One stone broke Francis' leg, and another knocked him out.

Then Slim held up Heimlich to distract the hungry bird.

"Yoo-hoo!" Heimlich called. "Mr. Early-bird, how about a nice, tasty worm on a stick?"

While the bird went after Heimlich, Flik and some of the other circus bugs worked together to rescue Dot and Francis. Heimlich almost got eaten by the bird, but he managed to hide. The bird turned back to Dot, Francis, and the bugs that had rescued them. The bird was in hot pursuit, but the bugs made it to a thorny bush just in time. They were safe at last!

Then Flik and the circus bugs heard a strange sound.

"What is that?" Rosie, the black widow spider, asked.

"That, my friends, is the sound of applause!" said Manny, the praying mantis.

After witnessing the triumphant rescue, Princess Atta apologized to Flik, and told him that he was very brave.

"Not every bug would face a bird," she said. "Even Hopper's afraid of 'em."

"Hopper's afraid of birds!" Flik said as an idea popped into his head.

Flik didn't think the Council would listen to him ever again, so he got the circus bugs to present his idea to the Council. The idea, Manny explained, was to build a fake bird to scare off Hopper. For once, the Council agreed to a new idea. They thought this one would work.

It took a lot of teamwork to build a life-sized bird. They used twigs and leaves for the body and feathers, and a nut for the beak. The ants enjoyed the job—they felt good about themselves for the first time in a long time.

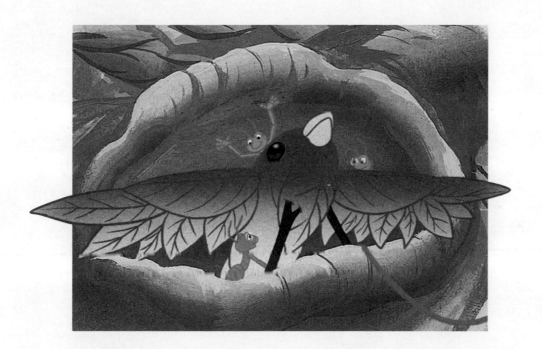

The circus bugs did their part, too. When the bird was constructed, they strung it up according to Manny's directions using Rosie's spider web. Then they hoisted it to the hollow of a tree, way up high. It would stay there until Hopper and his gang of grasshoppers arrived.

The ants all cheered as the bird was put into place. They knew that the next time the grasshoppers came, everything would be very different. This time, the ants would be prepared.

Meanwhile, south of the border, the grasshoppers were taking it easy. Some of them were too lazy to go back to Ant Island. They convinced Hopper's stupid brother Molt to say something to Hopper about it.

"Why go back?" Molt said. "You don't even like grain."

Hopper was furious. But he calmly turned to the other grasshoppers, pretending to agree with them.

"But there was that ant who stood up to me," Hopper said thoughtfully.

"We can forget about him," said one of the other grasshoppers.

"You let one ant stand up to us, then they all might stand up," Hopper said, letting his anger show.

Turning back to the other grasshoppers, he continued, "Those puny little ants outnumber us a hundred to one. And if they ever figure that out, there goes our way of life....Let's ride!"

And with that, the grasshoppers took off for Ant Island.

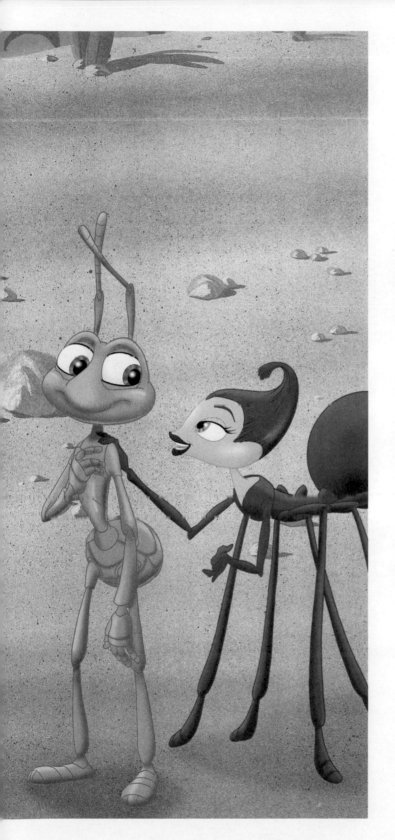

While the ant colony was having a party to celebrate finishing the bird, Flik took the circus bugs aside.

"When the party quiets down, I sneak you out the back way," he said, "and then you're outta here forever."

"Dim don't wanna go," the beetle said.

Rosie said that she would stay with Dim. None of the others wanted to leave either. They had made friends in the colony. Francis was even a den mother for Dot's Blueberry troop.

Then Princess Atta came up to them. "Will you look at this colony? I don't even recognize them!" she said. "And I have you bugs to thank for it, so thank you."

Just then, the alarm sounded. But it wasn't the grasshoppers who were arriving. It was P.T. Flea, looking for his circus bugs. Flik tried to cover up the poster he held up, but the ants easily recognized the bugs. They weren't warriors; they were a circus act!

The ants were furious at Flik for lying to everybody. The Queen ordered the circus bugs to leave, and Atta told Flik to go, too.

"And this time, don't come back," she said. Flik was devastated.

"Tough crowd," said P.T. as the circus carts pulled away with the gloomy bugs aboard.

Dot tried to follow Flik, but her mother wouldn't let her.

Then the last leaf fell—the moment of the grasshoppers' return. The ants panicked since they knew Hopper would never be satisfied with the amount of food they had collected.

"Mother, it's not enough," Atta said, worried. "What do we do?"

"I don't know," answered the Queen. They all trembled with fear as the alarm sounded. They knew that Hopper would be furious.

Hopper *was* furious. "Not one ant sleeps until we get every scrap of food on this island!" he shouted.

Hidden in a blade of grass, Dot and the other Blueberries overheard two of the grasshoppers talking about Hopper. "After the ants pick all the food," one said, "he's going to squish the Queen to remind 'em who's boss."

Dot knew she had to do something to save her mother. She told the other Blueberries to wait there, while she went to get help. She almost fell off a cliff when her tiny wings began to work—for the first time ever! She flew all the way until she caught up with Flik.

Flik didn't want to help at first, because he felt like such a failure. But the circus bugs encouraged him.

"We believe in you, my boy!" said Manny.

Then Dot gave him a stone to remind him of what he'd told her about a tiny seed growing into a big tree.

"All right, let's do it!" said Flik.

So the circus bugs tied up P.T. Flea and hijacked the circus carts to get back to the anthill. Flik's bird idea was finally going to fly.

Flik and Dot went to the hollow grass stalk to get the Blueberries, who were more than willing to help. Then they all climbed the tree where the fake bird was waiting.

Meanwhile, the circus bugs rode right up to where the grasshoppers were having a banquet with the Queen.

"Wait a minute!" Hopper said.

The bugs froze, except for Tuck and Roll, the pill bugs, who started their act. As they tumbled about, they got on each other's nerves, and soon they were fighting. Hopper laughed.

"Now that's funny!" he said, and settled in to watch the show.

Flik and the Blueberries had a bit of trouble getting the bird to fly, but soon they flew out of the hollow of the tree. From outside, the young ants' screams sounded a lot like a bird's screech.

When the grasshoppers looked up and saw the bird coming towards them, they all panicked and ran for cover. The circus bugs pretended to be injured by the bird. But P.T. Flea, who had managed to work his way free, didn't know about the plan.

P.T. saw his circus friends with fake blood on them and decided to go to their rescue. He lit a match, and held it up. The next time the bird swooped over him, it caught fire, causing it to crash-land. But the screams from inside did not stop. Flik and the Blueberries barely had time to escape the flames!

The last Blueberry out was Dot, and Hopper caught her.

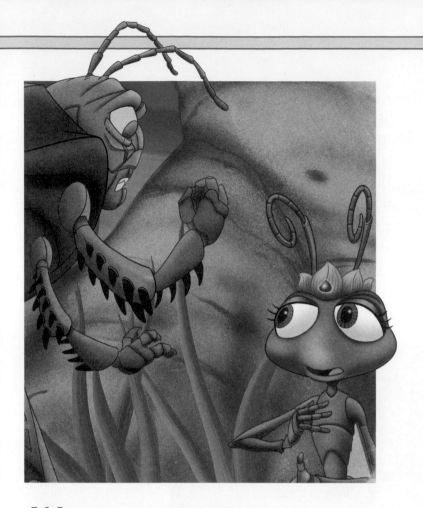

"Whose idea was this?" he asked Atta, pointing to the flaming bird. "Was it yours, Princess?"

Before Atta could answer, Flik stepped forward.

"Leave her alone, Hopper," he said. "The bird was my idea. I'm the one you want."

One of Hopper's goons jumped Flik and roughed him up before Hopper stopped him, to threaten the ants.

But Flik had something to say, too. "Year after year they somehow pick enough food for themselves and you," said Flik. "So who is the weaker species? Ants don't serve grasshoppers, it's you who need us!"

The crowd of ants and circus bugs murmured in agreement. They started to advance on the grasshoppers, who panicked and flew away—all except for Hopper. He glared at Flik with his most menacing stare. Then the first drops of rain began to fall.

As the ants scurried into the anthill to escape the huge raindrops, Hopper took advantage of the situation to grab Flik and fly away with him. But Princess Atta followed them. She managed to grab Flik and rescue him.

But Hopper was following close behind.

Flik had another idea. He told Atta to fly right towards the bird's nest! Hopper saw the bird looming overhead, but wasn't scared. "What's this?" he said. "Another one of your little bird tricks?"

"Yup," said Flik.

"Are there a bunch of little girls in this one, too?" asked Hopper. "Hello, girls!"

Flik smiled as Hopper realized too late that the bird was real. That was Flik's plan. The bird screeched as it went after Hopper and snatched him up in its beak.

With Hopper no longer a threat to the ant colony, it was time for the circus bugs to say goodbye. Francis tried not to cry as the Blueberries hugged him. Heimlich came out of his cocoon just in time.

"I'm a beautiful butterfly!" he cried, even though he didn't look very different. He now had tiny little wings that weren't even big enough to carry him, so Manny and Francis had to help him.

The newly crowned Queen Atta and the colony's official inventor, Flik, held hands as they waved goodbye to the circus bugs. And little Princess Dot made big plans for flying as much as her heart desired.